MORE PRAISE FOR

## THIS IS BETWEEN US

"*This Is* ... ut it
means t ... ry
everyon ... t
the cru ... ve
actually live. Kevin Sampsell has written the pieces of our
glorious failures and fleeting victories with such poignancy
my head and my heart are laughing, bleeding, and, above all,
dreaming onward. You want this book more than Facebook
and chocolate. I love it with my whole body."

**—LIDIA YUKNAVITCH**, author of *Dora: A Headcase*

"Kevin Sampsell is the original unadorned romantic. His
writing makes you love him, and it's easy all the way down.
*This Is Between Us* really DOES feel like you and he are
sharing these intimacies—sexy, honest moments that not
everyone is lucky enough to experience."

**—SUSIE BRIGHT**, author of *Big Sex, Little Death*

"Finely detailed and beautifully observed, *This Is Between Us*
captures the humorous and heart-wrenching intimacies of
two people in love. Kevin Sampsell sheds exquisite insight
into the way a hundred ordinary moments in a relationship
add up to something extraordinary and deeply meaningful.
This novel is moving, surprising, and utterly absorbing—I
couldn't put it down."

**—DAVY ROTHBART**, author of *My Heart Is an Idiot*

This is
between
us

# This is between us

A NOVEL BY
## KEVIN SAMPSELL

 TIN HOUSE BOOKS / Portland, Oregon & Brooklyn, New York

Published by Tin House Books, Portland, Oregon, and Brooklyn, New York

Distributed to the trade by Publishers Group West, 1700 Fourth St., Berkeley, CA 94710, www.pgw.com

Library of Congress Cataloging-in-Publication Data

Sampsell, Kevin.
This is between us : a novel / by Kevin Sampsell. — First U.S. edition.
    pages cm
 Distributed to the trade by Publishers Group West—T.p. verso.
 ISBN 978-1-935639-70-1
 1. Unmarried couples—Oregon—Portland—Fiction. 2. Single parent families—Oregon—Portland—Fiction. 3. Domestic fiction. I. Title.
 PS3569.A46647T45 2013
 813'.54—dc23

                         2013014878

Selections from this book originally appeared in the following publications: *Atticus Review, NANO Fiction, Spork, Hart House Review, Weekday,* the *Writers' Dojo, Fugue, Page Boy, Prism Index,* and *Smalldoggies Magazine.*

First U.S. edition 2013
Printed in the USA
Interior design by Jakob Vala
www.tinhouse.com

# YEAR ONE

The first time I went to your apartment, I wanted you to show me every room and demonstrate something you did in each one. "I like to imagine what you're doing all day when you're here," I said. "I like to think of you all the time," I said.

In the kitchen, I watched you make coffee. In the bathroom, you sat on the toilet seat for me. In the living room, you did some jumping jacks. You sat at the dining room table and ate a carrot while I watched you. In the bedroom, you slowly changed your clothes without taking your eyes off me.

...

We are both divorced, with one kid apiece. My son, Vince, was ten when we met. Your daughter, Maxine, was nine. We both have old school loans to pay. We couldn't remember exactly what we went to school for. We said things like, "Life gets in the way," and we laughed like it was a punch line.

...

We went to see a friend play music and there was only one chair left. I sat in it and you sat on my lap. We drank strong beer and felt the alcohol numb our blood. My legs fell asleep, and then I imagined that you were attached to me. There were eight legs— four wooden ones and four human ones, but two of the human ones were dead and useless. They just dragged on the ground. I imagined us wandering the aisles of a grocery store like that.

As I listened to the music—a grand and sweet and beautiful lilt—I read the label on the beer bottle and saw that the brewing company was founded in 1896. Then it felt like I was a mummy and you were a mummy. We were one drunken mummy, in love with our own wrapping.

...

When we first met, I became infatuated with your looks and I would project that infatuation onto strangers. I would see women about your height (five foot seven) and with your color hair (blonde) and with square librarian glasses and I'd want to follow them around to see if they walked like you, moved like you, or if their voice was like yours.

I would have fucked anyone who looked like you.

There was a time more recently when your hair was suddenly short and dark and my wandering eyes turned to women like that. When you weren't around I'd go to porn websites and search for porn stars who looked like you. It was a mix of fantasy and reality that I craved.

I watched a clip of a dark-haired woman with glasses performing oral sex on someone who was supposed to be her boss, in his office. Her hair was tied in two pigtails and the man had them in his hands, pulling her back toward him when she pulled away. I asked you to do that with your hair, but it wasn't as exciting as I'd hoped. I guess I didn't really want you to look like other people. I wanted other people to look like you.

. . .

I wonder how you described me to others. I wonder if you saw other guys who looked like me and felt like following them around. Did you objectify six-foot-tall dark-haired guys with glasses and receding hairlines? Did you really—as you implied once—like guys who were a little heavy? You said you liked my belly even though I could sometimes pinch three inches of it in my hand.

You said you liked it when I dressed up for my job at the hotel. You imagined me carrying your suitcases down a hallway to a top-floor suite and opening the door with a flourish. You'd enter the room and I would linger by the door and clear my throat, waiting for a tip. You wouldn't have cash.

You'd explain that you were a librarian and didn't have much money on you but you could pull some strings and eliminate any library late fees I had.

I'd watch your red-lipsticked mouth say the words *late fees*. I'd see your lips floating across the room, as if to kiss my lips, to say the words into my mouth—*Late fees late fees late fees* . . . you'd pull your glasses down a little and look at me over the frames as I imagined this fantasy inside a fantasy. Then I'd watch your eyes moving up and down my suit. You'd notice my right hand, still open and empty at my side. I'd start to say something but you'd put your finger to your lips, shushing me. Your fingernails also red, the color of STOP.

...

On just our second real date, we started talking about what our life together would be like. We talked about houses, careers, dreams, our kids, and our friends. Then we reluctantly talked about honesty, as if we weren't really sure what it meant.

"Will you tell me if you're attracted to someone else?" you said.

"I'm attracted to a lot of people," I said.

"But if you want to sleep with them?"

"I'll tell you if that happens," I said without thinking.

You took a long drink of your beer and looked around the restaurant.

"What about you?" I said. "Don't you find people attractive?"

"I do," you answered. "But there is always something wrong with them."

"What about us? There's gotta be something wrong with us."

"We're okay," you said. "We're perfect somehow."

The waiter came to our table and asked us about dessert. He seemed insistent about it, as if he knew we were trying to cultivate a romance. We noticed he had bad breath but ordered a mousse anyway.

"If I ever have bad breath, will you please tell me?" I said after he walked away.

"Okay," you said. "You mean starting right now?"

"Yes," I said, instinctively covering my mouth. "Even now."

"You have a little bit of a breath thing going on," you finally said.

"Thank you for being honest," I said.

...

My son, Vince, was droopy-eyed, sweet, a kid with soft, almost chubby edges. He wore friendship bracelets and always wanted to be useful. He hardly took naps after the age of four. He was a tornado with Legos and remote-control cars circling around him. He turned his attention later to skateboards and cop shows and European metal bands that released techno remixes. He sighed more, smiled less, as he got older. His black hair was a cowlick in front and a cowlick by his right ear. He hated his hair.

He was named after his mother's father, who used to like me but doesn't anymore. It's always strange when I see my former father-in-law now and call him by that name, the tension tightening the air around us.

...

It's something we joked about. Let's move in together and it will be like the Brady Bunch, but just two kids. We could all eat macaroni and cheese.

. . .

We synched our schedules with our exes so the kids would be at our apartment together more often than not. We fed them and made them give us good-night kisses. We clipped their nails at the same time on certain nights, with Nickelodeon on TV, because they were scared of things that cut. Because they seemed to trust us.

. . .

Your daughter, Maxine, was lanky, always leaning forward, with knees that she had to grow into. Her hair boyish and short, dirty blonde sometimes, brown and tawny in the colder months. She used her cell phone more than the rest of us. Sometimes she seemed too mean to be a kid. But she had a lot of friends, even though they seemed nervous around her. Or maybe they were nervous around us. She started wearing lipstick the same week she started wearing a bra. One friend of hers always smelled like cigarettes. The others smelled like perfume.

. . .

We were lying on the couch and you were talking about the food your mom used to make for you when you were growing up in Missouri. You asked me if I knew what Bunny Bread was and I said I didn't.

"Is it like sweet bread?" I asked.

"No, it's really probably-bad-for-you white bread."

"Oh, like Wonder Bread, then. That's what we had in the Northwest. Bright polka dots on the bag, like circus colors."

"Yeah, Bunny Bread is probably the same thing," you said. "My mom would make us really bad homemade chili with peanut butter sandwiches on Bunny Bread."

"What do you mean, *with*?"

"Like we were supposed to dip the sandwich in the chili. I guess it's a Midwest thing. I never liked it. I went on my first diet when I was eight and I never had it again."

"When you were eight?"

"Yeah, I couldn't eat what my mom was giving me. She didn't know how to cook. Her idea of eating healthier was to switch to wheat bread and diet soda."

"You ever taste Steak-umms?" I asked.

"Steak-whats?"

"It's like thinly sliced meat. Cooked in a pan, greasy and delicious and kind of gross at the same time. We used to eat it on Mondays."

"Why Mondays?" you asked.

"Because Spam was on Tuesdays," I answered.

"Did your family ever eat vegetables?"

"We had one onion in the freezer that my mom frugally shaved slivers from sometimes. I think that onion lasted for my whole childhood. Do potatoes count as a vegetable? I'm always confused about that."

"No," you said. "It's a tuber."

"I hate that word," I said.

You leaned back against me and lifted my arm to your mouth. You started chewing on it like it was corn on the cob.

...

When you took your shirt off for me the first time, I noticed the scar on your left nipple. I kissed your right breast and carefully cupped your left breast. You didn't seem shy about it, so I thought about asking you what happened, but decided not to yet. I wondered what other men before me had done. Did they talk to you about it right away? Were they turned off? Did they awkwardly apologize? I also wondered what you'd want me to do. Ask you about it? Ignore it? Maybe say it's beautiful and give it extra attention?

My face rubbed across your chest and I opened my eyes to focus on the nipple. It didn't look like a surgery scar. I wondered if you'd had a pierced nipple and maybe a stud or ring had been torn out during some horrible accident. I took my mouth off your right nipple and softly licked around your left. I waited for a few seconds to see if you'd stop me or flinch. I thought about the time an old girlfriend made it a point to kiss the mole on my back.

"Does that feel good?" I finally whispered.

"More than good," you answered, and your hand went up to my head, fingers spreading through my hair.

I covered your left nipple with my mouth, felt it with my tongue. I gave it a tender suck and felt something bloom there. I took my mouth off for a second and saw that the nipple was hard and alive, like the right one. I leaned back a moment and admired them both. They were matching now, moving hypnotically with your breathing.

Later, I said something to you about it. You didn't know

what I was talking about. "Your left nipple is shy," I said. "It doesn't stick out like the other one. I had to coax it out."

"I never noticed it like that before," you said.

I started to think I was wrong about it. Like maybe I was seeing things or having some kind of anxiety about how much attention I paid to your breasts. I never noticed the nipple receding after that. They were both so proud and hard. Sometimes I objectified them and thought of them as separate from your body. I imagined your breasts doing other things like driving a car, typing on a computer, or buttering toast. I wanted to give them names. Perky and Pokey. Betty and Boop. You and You. Mine and Mine.

. . .

You wanted to do it from behind, but I said I wanted to see your eyes. We hadn't seen each other for several days.

This was when we were both married to other people.

The passenger seat was pushed back and reclined. We were in your car, parked by the train tracks. It was far away from any busy street, so it was private enough. An abandoned warehouse gave us a little shield on one side, even though anyone on the passing cargo trains could see us easily. Maybe we were giving some hobos and conductors a show. But it was cold outside and our heat fogged up the windows.

You straddled me and wiped a clear spot on the window next to us so you could watch the trains passing. We could feel the vibration of their heavy loads, with names of companies like Bekins and Burlington Northern scrolling by. Elaborate graffiti of distorted faces and taggers' names decorated many of the cars. The windows kept fogging, so you reached up and opened the sunroof. You stuck your head out and for a second I could imagine the Headless Horseman riding on top of me. I heard you gasp and say, "There's someone over there."

"Where?" I said. "Is he coming over here?"

"He's just standing there, about a hundred feet away," you said. "But he's watching us."

The way you kept moving told me that the person didn't bother you too much. I tried to imagine what it looked like to that person—a small trembling Subaru with a woman's head sticking out of the top. Half woman, half car.

But maybe the person couldn't see us very well. It was pretty dark out and the only illumination came from some of the blinking red lights by the tracks.

You slowed down to a grind and we both came. You weren't saying anything but I could see your breath puffing out of your mouth like a steam whistle.

You slid back into the car and closed the sunroof and turned the key in the ignition. You laughed a little and said, "That was treacherous."

I nervously pulled my pants back on and looked out the window to see if the man was still around. "I wonder if that guy called the cops," I said. "We could get busted for public indecency."

You drove away calmly and quietly with a smile on your face and your shirt still unbuttoned. I saw my sweat drying on your chest. A few minutes later you said, "He had his dick out." The way you said it, I couldn't tell if you were excited or repulsed.

• • •

"I've never hated saying good night more than I do with you," I texted you the next night.

"You feel that way, too?" you replied.

"Yes. It's too much like good-bye and I never want to say good-bye to you," I texted back.

A minute later, you texted, "I know. It's depressing the way dinner is depressing."

I laughed about that but didn't know if you were joking or not. I wondered if you would be depressed every time we ate dinner. It didn't seem like a good state of mind to deal with every night for the rest of our lives.

"Let's just say Happy Easter or Merry Christmas or Happy Halloween instead of saying good night or good-bye," I texted.

"I like Halloween the best," you replied.

"Okay," I responded. "Happy Halloween."

Twenty minutes later you texted, "Happy Rosh Hashanah."

• • •

One night, you said you just wanted us to be friends. I was trying to be understanding but felt like I was on the defensive. This was over the phone, with the added frustration of not being able to see you or touch you.

"That's okay," I said. "But I will still want to tell you that I love you."

"No," you said. "Don't even do that."

"I just think it's dumb when people don't say what's in their heart," I said. "I know things will get better for us, even if we have to wait for months or years to work it out. To be together."

You didn't say anything. Your silence almost had an angry hum to it.

Finally, I said, softly, "I just don't believe in saying never."

You answered back, "But I want to say never."

"What?" I said, not sure of what I'd heard.

"I want to say never," you said again.

. . .

I wish I could make you magically appear before me whenever I want you. Do I just want to know where you are at all times? I ask myself twenty questions that are all answered by yes. Do I love you? Do I enjoy being with you? Do you make me anxious and frustrated? Do I want to die with you?

Here is a puzzle: If you were to move halfway around the world, to China or Pakistan, wouldn't we also be living half-a-day apart, so many miles and so much time separating us? If it were three in the morning there and three in the afternoon here, I would probably assume you were asleep. My mind could rest easy and not race with concerns about you doing something to hurt me. But if it were the other way around, I probably wouldn't be able to sleep because I'd be wondering what you were doing there, who you were seeing, and what you were wearing. I wonder what the difference between love and control is, but I'm afraid to look those words up in a dictionary.

Do you wonder about these things too?

Do you want a machine that'll make me appear before you whenever you want?

Do I make you anxious and frustrated? When you're with me, do you want to take fewer pills or more pills?

Do you want me to go to bed at a certain time, wearing a full set of pajamas?

Do you want to monitor me with an electronic ankle bracelet?

Do you want to smell me when I get home, the same way I want to smell you when I come home from work?

Do you think of me when you're shelving books at the library?

Do I make you laugh? In a good way, I mean.

Do you love me?

Did you answer yes to all of these?

I remember once you told me that it was hard to say no to me. We always seem to float toward the *yes* in any situation, without thinking too much about it. But should we be more careful? More under control?

What should we do with our urges?

...

You picked me up for lunch one day and I could see you'd been crying. Your divorce had finally gone through. The bill was in an envelope between us. An open bottle of anxiety pills sat in one of the cup holders. You told me to look at the bill. "Tell me the damage," you said.

The envelope was nice, a lightly textured paper that reminded me of bleached teeth, and the law office name looked regal in the left corner. I pulled out the bill and saw that it was for $2,900. Moneywise, this wasn't good timing. We both had a lot of debt at this point, as well as a new dentist bill, a speeding ticket, and overdue credit cards. You'd even checked out a book at the library about how women's emotional distress leads to money problems. You said you couldn't read for pleasure anymore.

"Tell me it'll be okay," you said.

"It's okay," I said.

"But it's not okay right now," you said. "I'm fine with that. I'm dealing. I just want to know that things *will* be okay. In the future. Like, someday when the library gives me a decent pay raise."

I held your hand and watched your eyes turn bright and wet again. "It's funny," you said. "The more I watch Maxine grow up, the less I think about myself. I can fake my well-being. I can live hungry. I can take on a shitload of problems. I just can't stand the thought of her having an unhappy childhood."

"I know what you mean," I said, although I wasn't sure if I had the same willingness to sacrifice.

...

The first time I met your brother, Daniel, I could tell he was checking me out, sizing me up. You had told me that he was hard to predict. When you were just starting college, he had already stolen two of your boyfriends and had even tried to seduce one of your dad's friends. But he also took you out to dinner and talked to you whenever you were having problems. He loaned you money often. He gossiped about guys with you. He brought you soup and flowers when you were home sick.

"You get to stay at the hotel for free whenever you want?" he asked me. We were at a restaurant that he had chosen. It was too expensive for us, so we just had appetizers and water. He sat on the other side of the table and you held my hand on your lap, where he couldn't see.

"No," I told him. "But we do get one free weekend a year if we need it. And discounts."

He laughed a little, more like a smirk. It took a while, but we found something to talk about over the cheese and bread plate—boxing. He was a big Mike Tyson fan. "I like his voice," he said. "I like how he beat people in the first round all the time."

Under the table, I accidentally brushed my foot against his leg. He didn't flinch at all.

. . .

We had the drug conversation one night. I'd only had this talk with a couple of other past girlfriends and my ex-wife. It made me feel the same way that the question *How many people have you slept with?* makes me feel. It's almost like asking someone how much indescribable pleasure they've had in their life. One past girlfriend went on for so long about how much she liked ecstasy that I started to feel like I could never measure up.

One ex told me that she never did drugs, but I eventually found out that she was an alcoholic. Another one didn't count the antidepressants that she almost overdosed on six months later. My first girlfriend was addicted to Lucky Charms cereal (she would keep a Ziploc bag of it in her purse).

You told me you used to like cocaine but switched to pills when your dealer got busted. You gave me a long list of the pills and I had heard of only a couple of them. You described the different combinations you'd tried, the various effects. But you also said you were trying to become more healthy. You were running, doing yoga, buying crossword puzzle books, and watching more documentaries.

All the documentaries you watch are about drugs.

...

Moving in with someone is like pruning yourself. Two people turning into a multilimbed, two-headed, two-hearted being. There were things to be considered, like colors (my mismatched dishes were given to Goodwill), bed sheets (yours didn't quite fit my bed), and food choices (everything with high-fructose corn syrup had to go).

Plus there were the kids, who were excited to live together, despite their lingering confusion. Just months before, they'd had both biological parents going to their teacher conferences, eating dinner with them, and tucking them in at night. I wondered if they sensed any of the cracking, the shifting, or the trepidation that was happening in us—you, me, our exes. We tried to "act normal." As if breaking vows happened every day. You asked me, "Do you think we're sending the wrong message by falling in love?" I didn't know how to answer that.

Maybe my perspective was a little skewed, but it looked like everything in the Goodwill pile was mine.

Formerly mine.

It felt like more you than me in our new place. We were both moving from our own cozy houses to a slightly cramped apartment. But by the next day I was okay with that.

Here we were: eight legs, eight arms, four hearts. Neatly packed in a white wooden box. Sometimes I stood outside and stared at the chimney on top, slowly puffing smoke.

. . .

As we started to figure out our new living together routine, I often wondered which one of us had a darker, gloomier spirit. You always wore black and listened to bands like Swans and Psychic TV. You had seen all the movies about serial killers and even showed me the YouTube video of the politician who shot himself in the head at a press conference.

I used to watch the *Faces of Death* movies and thought G. G. Allin was funny. I had a Joel-Peter Witkin photograph in my bathroom.

But ever since Vince was born, I had become surprisingly sensitive to some things. I was getting soft. Sentimental TV commercials would make me cry. If a movie was sexually suggestive, I'd turn it off until he wasn't around. If someone was using bad language at a basketball game, I'd ask the person to stop. I was suddenly a concerned dad. Mr. Clean. A polite papa. I was responsible for a son. And now, in a lot of ways, for Maxine, too.

But when we were alone, after the kids were sent to bed, we let our dark spirits out—and they came out with a vengeance. Like they had been repressed all day long, forced to watch the Disney Channel and read *The Velveteen Rabbit* out loud.

We drank and swore and made sexist and racist jokes about everything on the late news. I'm not even sure if you could say irony was present in these jokes. We'd unload them like it was a competition. If you said something offensive, I had to one-up you. We laughed a good long time and turned the TV back to the kids' station before turning it off. We went to bed, and in the morning we woke up clean again.

...

When we first met, you were still married but separated from your husband. It was not the ideal circumstance, but it's the one we found ourselves in. You told me he still loved you but your feelings for him had changed for some unknown reason. His name was Sage, and he would send you gifts and leave messages for you. You didn't want to tell him to stop because you secretly liked it. But deep inside, you knew that you couldn't love Sage in the same way.

I often wondered if I would be in his position someday.

But I had no right to think that. I was also married when we met and my feelings for my wife had changed, too. I never told anyone exactly why, but it came down to one thing: disappointment. I became disappointed in her and I was disappointed in myself. Our relationship was infected with disappointment. It ate away at me.

You and I found each other and tried to run away from our poisons and sadness. You looked for freedom. I looked for escape. Once a leaver, always a leaver. Sometimes I feel like we're just keeping an eye on each other.

. . .

You have a locket that holds a photo of you with your brother and mom and dad. You're nine years old and your hair is in a ponytail that juts up behind you, just under your dad's chin. You have other lockets with old photos in them too. You with your best friend, you with your family dog, you with Santa Claus.

I asked you why you don't have lockets with current photos in them. "Because these are like treasures," you said. "Because I admire the innocence in these pictures. Because I like to wear them close to my heart. Because people are always curious what I was like before now."

I gave you a locket with an old photo of me, from when I was about fifteen. "I like this so much," you said, tracing your finger around the photograph. "I feel like this answers a lot of questions for me. Like I knew you then, even if I didn't."

. . .

I had a little red bump on my cheek, right under my eye, and you said you could lance it off. I was scared by the word *lance*, but you said it was okay, that you did it all the time.

"I've had these before," you said. "It's just a little seed."

It did feel like a little seed in there. At first I thought it was a pimple but it never went away. It had been on my face for almost three months.

"It's not like a cancer thing, is it?" I asked.

"No," you said. "You'd probably be dead by now if it were."

I wasn't sure if you were joking. Probably not, since cancer wasn't really a jokey thing with you. You always wore a hat outside because, you said, you didn't want the sun to give you skin cancer on your head. You didn't seem concerned about the sun hitting you anywhere else. "The head is very prone to bad things," you once told me.

"I can feel it in there," you said, touching my bump. I put my finger on it too and imagined it looked like a sesame seed.

I saw you searching your purse and then you pulled out something that I hadn't seen before. It looked like an X-ACTO knife. "You just carry that around with you everywhere?" I said. My body was tensing up.

"Let me get a hot cloth on it first," you said. You went to the bathroom and I heard the water running. I figured I had about forty-five seconds to think of an alternative. When you came back, I saw a bounce in your step. You pressed the hot towel to my face and smiled. I asked if we should numb it somehow but you laughed and said, "This will be fine."

I felt the small blade press into the bump. "Here it comes," you said. You stopped for a second and then reached over and grabbed your glasses to put on, like a doctor protecting her eyes. There was a little blood and a gentle scratching with the blade and then you reached up and caught it with your finger. When you showed it to me, it looked like a small, perfect pearl.

It wasn't what I expected. "Back to normal," you said, and then you squished it in your fingers and pretended to eat it.

...

We took the kids out to the pumpkin patch. We'd been together for about a year, but Vince and Maxine were still getting used to being around each other. If we didn't plan activities, like going to the zoo, the park, or a movie, they'd grow restless and uneasy and squabble. This was a slight strain on our relationship but it gave us something to talk about when we felt dull or tired.

One long-bed tractor gave all the parents and their kids a ride out to a large corn maze by the pumpkin patch. Each year the maze was cut into a different image that could be seen only from an aerial view. One year it was the shape of Oregon with a duck and a beaver in the middle. This particular year it was supposedly the image of Lewis and Clark. "How do they make the shapes?" Vince asked us. We didn't know and frankly it hurt to think about. I tried to make a joke about aliens, but Maxine didn't like the joke and said something about alien abductions.

Another tractor took us and a few other people out to the bumpy fields where pumpkins riddled twenty acres. We sat on bales of hay as the driver went slow, sometimes turning around to make sure we were all safe and smiling. You looked like a farm girl, so I took a picture of you with a disposable camera.

After the tractor engine was turned off and the brake was set, the four of us scattered to find our own pumpkins.

"How can you tell which one is the best?" Maxine asked.

"As long as it's orange and shaped like your head," I told her.

Everyone grabbed pumpkins that were shaped amazingly like their heads. I was the only one who broke my own rule. Mine was a fifteen-pounder shaped like a heart. Not a valentine heart, but an actual heart.

We walked back to the spot where the tractor would pick us up again. The air was crisp and full of warm voices and laughter. The sun, low and gleaming, made our shadows long in front of us. "Look at our shadows," I said. We raised our arms up and made the shape of a crown. Then we put our pumpkins on our shoulders and stood together to make an eight-headed creature. We laughed and then stood apart from each other and made our shadows hold hands.

You looked at me and said, "I like our shadows."

...

"I want to see you dressed like David Bowie," you said.

"For Halloween?" I asked.

"No," you said. "For the bedroom."

"Keep going," I said.

"I want to see you with seventies space shoulder pads and gold tights with leather platform boots."

"What about my hair?"

"Big and poofed up, like a lion!"

"Like in *Labyrinth*?" I tried to remember if I liked that movie.

"Who do you want me to dress up like?" you asked.

I had to pretend like I was thinking about it, but the truth is I'd had the answer to this question in my head for most of my life. Still, I tried to play it a little vague.

"Um, I can't remember her name," I started, "but she's on an album cover from the seventies and she's wearing roller skates, striped athletic socks up to her knees, short shorts, a white T-shirt, and a satin letterman jacket."

"You want me to dress up like Linda Ronstadt on the cover of her album *Living in the USA*?"

You seemed weirdly happy and excited about this. "And she had knee pads too," I said.

You squinted your eyes at the ceiling fan, like its spinning above us was your brain working out a plan. "This might get complicated," you said.

. . .

Instead of a bomb threat, you called me at work with a sex threat. You disguised your voice, scrambled your number. Made promises. I was working at the front desk and I had just checked in a tall, beautiful redhead with breast implants. I was thinking about what you would look like with breast implants when you called.

I hung up the hotel phone, shaking and a little aroused. I went into the bathroom and took a picture of my cock with my cell phone. I sent it to you but you didn't reply. An hour later, I sent you a picture of my mouth. You sent me a text that said, "Mixed message."

I tried to think of something else to take a picture of. I wondered to myself, *What's more exciting than a cock and a mouth?* I took off my shirt and snapped a picture of my left breast, where my heart lives. I looked at the photo and realized that my nipple looked disgusting. It didn't look round to me. It looked like a flat tire, deserted in a bed of black weeds.

I took another photo and it was blurry, which made it worse. I found a red marker and drew a heart shape around my nipple. I colored it in, then took another picture. I felt like a tart. I felt like a clown.

Ten minutes later, you sent me one like it, but much better. It wasn't even lunchtime yet. How could I work under those circumstances?

...

We drove up to Bellingham and spent a weekend at your sister's house with the kids and it was one of those houses where we had to take off our shoes. This No Shoes in the House rule bothers me. I wanted to walk around with my shoes on until they said something, but they would probably just twist their faces into concerned looks.

Before dinner, I decided to shave. I had to use one of your sister's razors and it kept cutting me. I was bleeding near my Adam's apple and on both of my cheeks. I decided to give up before I cut myself more. I came out with a scraggly goatee surrounded by red smears. Your sister's seven-year-old son watched me as I ate and dabbed at the cuts every few minutes. Her husband was out of town and it was a quiet dining room without him. I apologized about my bad shaving and the boy said he wanted to shave now too. Vince and Maxine said we should play barber shop after dinner. I took your sister's shaver and lathered the kids up. With the plastic guard covering the razor, I swiped all the shaving cream off, pretending to be very careful and professional the whole time. I took a red pen and made a mark on Vince like he was nicked. Then all the kids wanted that. "I want a blood mark too," your sister's son said.

And then suddenly, as if incited by the sight of our own fake blood, we were savages. We tromped around the house in our slippery socks and clean-shaven bloody faces. We were armed with blunt plastic toys. Grown-ups versus kids. We let the kids win.

. . .

One time, when I was eleven, I walked in on my parents when they were having sex. They were doing it doggy style, and my mom's heavy breasts swung back and forth between her locked elbows. I made some kind of sound, a surprised groan maybe, and they noticed me in the door. My mom collapsed flat but my dad kept going on her. I locked eyes with him for a few seconds and he slowed himself to a frustrated stop. And then my mom said, "Honey, can you go to the store and get a loaf of bread?" She was trying to cover herself but my dad stayed defiant and naked, only his groin shielded.

"Okay," I told my mom.

"There's a five-dollar bill in my purse," she said.

Her purse was on their dresser on the other side of their bedroom. I walked across, looking away from them, and unzipped her purse to root around for the money. It was very quiet now. I snuck a sideways glance and saw that my dad was wearing light blue socks that came to his knees. "Okay," I said again.

"You can buy a candy bar for yourself too," she said.

I left the room and walked down the hall. I went to the front door and opened and shut it loudly. But I stayed inside the house and listened.

...

I remember on one of our first dates, when we were at the park and no one else was there, you got on your hands and knees and pretended to be a dog. You smiled and panted and barked up at me. You were trying to make me laugh. "I wish we had a leash," you said.

I petted you with pride.

...

Vince and I have something called DTYM. It stands for Don't Tell Your Mom. She can be very sensitive and judgmental about things.

If we watch a rated-R movie or a show that might be too scary, it's a DTYM. If I give him secret driving lessons in the mall parking lot, it's a DTYM. Sometimes we'll be watching stand-up comedy on YouTube and the material will turn raunchy. "Is this a DTYM?" Vince will ask.

When I gave him the talk about sex, when I told him that his penis can make babies and that girls bleed between their legs once a month, he looked uneasy, like he was in trouble for something.

"I'm just telling you these things so you know," I said. "Do you have any questions or anything?"

He looked like he wanted to say something but didn't.

"How's your penis?" I said. "I mean, is everything okay down there? When you take a shower, do you wash it good?" This was actually a question I had wanted to ask him for a long time because of his foreskin.

"Yes," Vince said.

"That's good," I said. "It feels good to wash it, you know?" I looked him in the eyes when I said this, although maybe I shouldn't have. Maybe it was too weird. But he had been taking long showers, sometimes twice a day, and I wanted him to know that it was okay.

"Is this a DTYM?" he asked me.

"Sure," I said. "Sure thing."

...

It was last call and we were much too drunk to drive. We were in a strip club where the walls were lined with huge tanks full of piranhas. We paid all the dancers to feed them in front of us. This meant they took a pitcher of water with a couple of goldfish in it and climbed a jungle-style rope ladder about ten feet above us and dropped them in. We watched a lot of flesh get naked and torn apart that night.

I ordered coffees in an attempt to sober us up enough to drive but the bartender brought us Irish coffees instead, heavy on the whiskey. It was snowing heavily outside, so we had no choice but to walk home. We slipped and fell down so much that we started to look like yetis, covered in white from head to boot. I stood guard while you squatted down and somehow peed a heart shape in the snow. It shined like gold under the streetlamps. You watched for cops while I made an arrow through it.

...

When Vince was born, at home with midwives, my ex-wife and I did not have him circumcised. I'm not really sure why we didn't. I was a circumcised Catholic and his mom was an ex-Catholic. I always wondered if his mother was trying to make some kind of statement by not getting it done. Was it some kind of hippie thing? A way to keep him "natural" or something?

She had also not shaved her legs while she was pregnant.

Now, Vince's mom has remarried into a Jewish family. There was talk for a while about getting Vince circumcised so he could convert to Judaism properly, but somehow it was avoided.

I'm not sure why I didn't have it done when he was born. I sometimes wonder if other kids say anything to him about it, in the locker room or bathrooms at school. I always thought that the son's penis should look like his dad's penis. But my son has not seen my penis, so maybe he's unaware that we do not match.

I mentioned this to a friend recently and he laughed and said, "Why do you need to match? For the family photos?"

Still, I've grown to regret this.

...

We went to meet some friends at a concert in the zoo. There was a big outdoor stage and a young British singer sang an array of pop covers in a pseudo-jazz style. There was something forced about his appearance, his personality. We could tell he was short and not very attractive, but his hairstyle and vintage-looking suit gave him the appearance of a kid dressing up for his older sister's wedding.

"This is the kind of jazz that middle-aged soap opera viewers like," I said.

"This is the kind of jazz that white people on boats listen to when they're trying to attract a mate," you said.

"What kind of mate?" I wanted to know.

"An exotic one," you said. "White people on boats go for exotic more than anything."

"Like a girl who can't speak English very well?" I asked.

"That doesn't matter so much. I know a really beautiful Korean girl who has never been to Korea or spoken the language. As long as they look foreign. Japanese, Mexican, Creole. Anything with dark or freckled skin."

"Does Irish count? Redheads?"

"No, they don't count," you said.

We listened to the singer and watched everyone around us smiling, nodding their heads, off in their individual fantasies.

"I never had an Irish girl," I said.

"Let's walk around," you said.

We told our friends that we were going to get some beers and then we wandered off to where the animals were.

"I wonder what kind of animals Irish girls like," you said.

"I'm not really that interested," I said. "I mean, can you even name a hot Irish girl? Someone actually from the country?"

We wandered through the monkey house and stopped to watch two monkeys grooming each other very carefully.

No one else was around. The sound of the singer, crooning a Radiohead song, fluttered through the air.

...

You told me about the dead squirrel in the road and how much it bothered you. You were convinced that people hit animals on purpose, especially in our neighborhood. You talked about it the whole weekend but I couldn't figure out which road you were talking about. You started to get a migraine and didn't want to think about the squirrel anymore. I made you some chicken soup and massaged your head behind the ears. You turned off all the lights and lay on the couch, pinching the bridge of your nose.

I went out to the store to get you some medicine and on the way back I drove down the road where the squirrel was. It was right in the middle, where it wouldn't be hit unless someone swerved. I drove past but then decided to turn around. I pulled over and grabbed a small empty box that was in the trunk. I didn't want to touch the animal but I was able to scoop it up with the box. It didn't seem as stiff as I thought it would be. It was heavy and flopped around. I flung it under a bush on the side of the road and covered it with brown and orange leaves.

When I got home, you were up and doing yoga. You said you suddenly felt better. You said the pressure had just faded and gone away.

. . .

For some reason, this squirrel incident reminds me of a time when Vince and I were playing at a park, when he was about five years old. He brought some of his miniature Lego figures and was playing with them on the slide and by the swings. When we were on our way home, he couldn't find the little plastic sword that came with his Knight Guy. That's what he called them: guys. Ninja Guy. Police Guy. Cowboy Guy. Worker Guy. Knight Guy.

He was sad and wouldn't eat his dinner. I told him we could go look for the sword in the morning but he started crying and said, "He needs his sword tonight. He always sleeps with his sword."

I told him if he ate five bites of dinner we would go look for the sword. He ate his bites with a sad face and then we drove back to the park. It was already dark, so we brought flashlights. I didn't think we would find it—a gray piece of plastic barely an inch long. After ten minutes, though, I did find it. "Okay," I said. "No more losing Lego stuff at the park."

We drove back home, Vince strapped into his booster seat, worn out from the long day but happy and smiling, clutching his Knight Guy, who clutched his sword. It was one of the times I remember him being totally happy, totally at peace.

. . .

You came over to the hotel on your lunch break and we snuck into a room that I'd just checked someone out of. We made love quickly, then stayed, lying on the bed together. Our thighs were touching. We were looking at the ceiling, breathing heavy, then steady, then soft. We heard muffled music from another room. Something romantic and soulful.

"We're like, in love," you said.

"Yep. We're in the middle of it," I said.

"We really are. We're, like, in love."

"You say it like you just realized that," I said, and looked over at you.

"I did!" Your eyes lit up when you said this, growing big like overinflated balloons.

"What do you mean?"

"Like, I knew I loved you. And I knew you loved me. But I didn't realize that we were *in* love."

I found myself fully and emotionally engulfed in the moment. I had twenty-five minutes left on my lunch break. I counted the minutes up instead of counting them down.

...

I'm spinning a loaf of bread on my fingers. Will you dance with me next? The sun is on our naked backs.

# YEAR TWO

The park down the street is "our park."

The old man who works in his garden three houses down is "our old man."

The café where we get pumpkin scones on Tuesday mornings is "our café." Those scones are "our scones."

That song by Fleetwood Mac is "our song" and so is that one by LL Cool J.

I took my friend Sarah to the auto parts store on Eighty-Second Avenue so she could get a new battery for her car. You seemed upset when I told you, but you said that nothing was wrong. Finally, before we went to bed, you said, "I can't believe you took her to *our* auto parts store."

...

We forgot about nature sometimes. In the park, lying in the grass, it felt perfect and peaceful. The grass was so green, almost garish. It seemed exotic.

"Come over here and feel this," you said.

I lifted my head to see you by a tall knobby tree. "I've touched a tree before," I said.

"When was the last time you touched a tree?" you asked.

"Probably last week." I shrugged.

"I doubt it," you said.

You were right. We see trees all the time but never touch them.

I got up and pressed my hands on the tree, like I was searching for a heartbeat.

"Keep them there," you said. You looked around to see if anyone was watching and then you started carving our initials into it.

...

I liked the gaps in you. The top of your shirt billowing open for my own peep show when you bend down to tie your shoes. The smooth skin space between the bottom of your shirt and the buttons on your Levi's when you reached up for something in the kitchen cabinet. The gap between your front teeth. The thin delicate bridge between your toughness and sadness.

I would watch you walking up the stairs ahead of me and concentrate on the bottoms of your feet clapping against your flip-flops.

...

It was Sheryl, my ex-wife, who taught me to go slow in bed. I was a jackrabbit. That's what she whispered to her friends.

One of her friends told me that later. Or maybe it was a *jack-hammer*. A handful of thrusts and it was over, like I was in a race.

I'm not sure where this method came from, but I was quick to blame a weekly circle jerk I had with friends when I was in tenth grade. We took turns having sleepovers, lugging our smelly sleeping bags from basement to basement. Rusty zippers always getting stuck. To cut down on possibly incriminating evidence, we could use only one piece of stimulation—like a page from *Sports Illustrated*'s swimsuit issue, a banana peel, or massage oil. Sometimes we traded panties and bras from our moms' or sisters' dressers. This little private club lasted from Christmas break to summer vacation and then we all went to summer camps and grew apart.

For a long time, I was a speed demon and knew no other way. I could summon a handful of sticky in twelve seconds. I didn't think about how this eventually affected my girl-friends. I thought me coming = them coming too. Their fingers were usually called on to finish my unfinished job. I'd lie there, exhausted, and watch their faces change as their bodies squirmed next to me.

When I met Sheryl, she was just as inexperienced as I was, but she read magazines and had some strategic ideas of her own.

Her best one was the candle trick. She would put lit candles on the headboard of the bed frame. The surface there was only about five inches wide, so if the bed jostled too much, the candles would fall over. Night after night, I would watch the small lineup of flames nervously as I moved inside her.

When I was close to climax, I would be tempted to go faster but I had to be careful. For a couple of months, I couldn't even look at her face for more than a few seconds. My brain would play tricks on me. I'd see flames growing tall out of the corner of my eyes. I imagined the bed going up in flames at the same time as my premature ejaculation.

Eventually I mastered the slower speed, the steady pace of delicious friction and heat. I could watch Sheryl's face and breasts and hips again. They glowed in the dark.

...

If I flipped over and put my back to you in bed, I called this "cooking the other side." I called it this because I imagined myself as a big piece of meat on a grill. On some nights, I had to flip over continually until I was more comfortable (evenly cooked).

I also liked how it felt when you put your back to me at the same time. We called this "butt to butt."

There were some nights when you lost your patience with me and would ask me to face you for a good-night kiss, and I'd say, "Hold on a minute. I have to finish cooking this one side."

...

I told you that I still loved all my past girlfriends.

"How many is that?" you asked.

"Well, probably not all of them," I said. "But five or six for sure."

You turned your eyes from me and I could see your shoulders drop.

I tried to explain it further. "Love is fluid, I think. It doesn't follow timelines. Once it starts, it doesn't end or anything. I mean, it might stop growing but maybe it just buries itself inside of you when a relationship ends. So, like, you can dig it up again if you want to. All of those exes contributed in different ways to make me who I am now. Same with you and your ex-boyfriends. If you never went out with John, you would have never learned to like cool music."

"I'll always appreciate John for that," you said. "But can't you just be thankful?"

"That's part of the love," I said.

"I always think about who will be at my bedside when I'm dying," you said. "What if all of my ex-boyfriends were there?"

I wasn't sure what to think about that. "Are they nice?" I finally asked. "I mean, do you love them?"

"I did," you said. "But what's the point of that? The hospital room can only fit so many people. Are they all going to huddle around me and try to hold my hand? I'm claustrophobic. Besides, that's what the funeral is for."

"So you just want me there?" I asked.

You answered back quickly. "I don't want anyone else to see me die. It will be our own private moment."

. . .

We went to see an ex-boyfriend of yours play in a band at Berbati's. It was about a year after we started going out. I had never met the ex-boyfriend before, but I knew he was the one you went out with before you got married and had Maxine. You said the relationship was a good one, but then he moved to Seattle to play bass in this band. You said the breakup was "reluctant" at the time. His name was Peter.

It was a slow night at the bar, with only twenty or so other people there for the show. This made me feel good for some reason, that his band wasn't popular.

You pointed him out to me while the opening band played. He didn't look so great, which also made me feel more comfortable.

When they got on stage though, the guy you had pointed at sat behind the drums and another, taller and better-looking young man picked up the bass.

"Is Peter the drummer?" I asked you.

"No. I told you he plays bass."

I looked at the bass player and realized I must have misread your pointing finger earlier. We watched the band's set of aggressive noise-rock as I felt a knot in my stomach getting tighter. I remembered you once told me that you were turned on at rock shows because you thought the way musicians played their instruments must be the same way they had sex. You could see the passion in their faces and in their tensed muscles, you had told me.

After the show, we talked with the old boyfriend while the band packed up their gear and you bought one of their CDs. We drank a beer with him and then you hugged him for a couple of seconds longer than I expected.

"Peter is a pretty good-looking guy," I said on the drive home.

"You sound surprised," you said.

"He looks young," I said.

You didn't say anything.

"How old is he?" I asked.

"He's seven years younger than me," you said. "Don't be a dick."

"I heard that it's hard to date guys in bands." My voice unexpectedly cracked.

"I don't know," you said. "I'm not dating a guy in a band."

. . .

One night, I saw an old girlfriend at a bar and made out with her in the unisex bathroom. I reached inside her shirt and felt the heavy weight of her breasts. She touched me through my pants and made me come. I told her I wanted to make her come too, but she just laughed and asked me to buy her another drink instead.

I got home two hours later than I said I would. I went into the neighbors' yard and peed in their bushes and then tore some flowers out of their garden. I rested them on your pillow and fell quickly asleep.

. . .

You were arranging the flowers I'd brought home to you in a tall vase. You had pricked your finger on a thorn and it was bleeding so softly and quietly. You didn't ask me what the occasion was.

. . .

You told me that you used to spy on your parents when you were in seventh grade. You and your brother, Daniel, who is about three years older than you, sometimes took turns peering through a secret peephole that he had made in his closet. It was tiny, but you could see a little bit of their bed and the reflection of a big mirror on their dresser.

"I wanted to look all the time," you told me. "But Daniel said he would only do it when he was bored. He also said not to come in his room when he wasn't home, but I still did it. I would be quiet and I would get in there, behind his hangers and his clothes."

I asked if that was how you learned about sex. "Yes, probably. But sometimes it would be too dark to see anything. I'd only be able to listen and guess what was happening." You closed your eyes tight, trying to remember.

Your parents were probably our age or younger when you were spying on them. I imagined you, twelve years old, a cute mess of knees and elbows and long hair. And then I could see Maxine in the closet and you and me reflected off that mirror.

"I was so happy to see them that way," you said. "The peephole was so small that it gave everything I saw a fuzzy edge, like when they used to smudge Vaseline on camera lenses. I could tell they had romance and passion and it gave me this elevated sense of hope for the future. But maybe even more than that, I was turned on."

You stopped and exhaled, as if you'd been holding your breath in. You looked at me and then quickly away.

"Do you think it turned your brother on too?" I asked.

"I think so," you said. "He tried to hide it, but it did. Sometimes we would both cry while watching them. I'd wipe my eyes with the sleeve of one of his shirts because I wanted to seem like I was more cool or something. But he could see that my eyes were red. We were a close family that way. It was secret and it was magic."

...

Tragedy keeps us grounded. If things are going well for too long, we get suspicious. But still, we don't know how to act when something bad happens. We accidentally laughed when our friend told us about her dead bird. When Maxine got her first period and cried, I cried too.

...

Sometimes we try to make sad things beautiful. One night, my cock was an airplane and your legs were the Twin Towers. I held them up and watched the plane land smoothly between them, over and over.

...

Sometimes I'd roll the passenger-side window all the way down and take my foot off the brake and creep forward next to the sidewalk in our neighborhood, and Vince would jog alongside for a few seconds before dramatically jumping in through the open window. Like *Starsky and Hutch*, I said. He didn't get the reference but still thought it was funny.

"DTYM," I would say, and he would laugh because he knew it was a ridiculous stunt that would be too hard to explain to his mom anyway.

For a while it was his favorite thing to do and we did it for about six months before he had a growth spurt and was getting too big for the window. "*Starsky and Hutch*," he'd say, and I'd roll down the window.

One time, Maxine was with us and he wanted her to do it with him. "I'll go first," he said.

I wanted to say it wasn't a good idea. I wanted to be a responsible adult. But I said, "Just this once."

"I'm Starsky," Maxine said. She was laughing so hard she almost couldn't do it. I slowed almost to a stop as she flopped through the window with Vince pulling her in.

"We did it!" Vince shouted. Then he gave me a soft punch on the arm. "Step on it, Dad. Go!"

I pushed the car to a steady twenty-five miles per hour.

...

"I think we all want to kill our children at some point," you said while falling asleep on one of our first nights together.

We'd been talking in the dark about parenting for two hours, most of it positive. Then we were finally fading. There was that sleepy silence and then those words, groggy and slurred, like maybe they weren't meant to be heard at all. But it was the kind of statement that only parents would know was true—something that most parents have thought about, but then laughed uncomfortably to themselves while thinking it. I knew how brave you were then, or at least how brave your honesty was.

. . .

I was away for ten days, visiting family in Washington. I wished I were back at home with you, lounging around in underwear and socks, watching a movie after the kids went to bed. You suggested that we watch a movie together, over the phone. You had a copy of *Say Anything* at home already, so I went out and rented a copy from the video store down the street from where I was staying.

I called you back and we synched up our movies. We paused on the first frame of the movie studio logo. "Got it ready?" you asked me.

I counted down from five to zero and then we pressed play. We could hear each other's television, the dialogue and music echoing together through the wires. We talked quietly, like we were sitting right next to each other on the couch. "I like the way her dad looks at him in this dinner scene," I said. During the scenes where Lili Taylor sang songs about her ex-boyfriend, Joe (*Joe Lies!*) we sang along.

When John Cusack swept broken glass out of Ione Skye's path, I could hear a romantic sigh come from your mouth.

We had a running competition to see who could name the various Seattle landmarks when they appeared on-screen.

During the boom box scene, we shouted back and forth to each other, "Yes!" "Yes!" "Yes!" as Peter Gabriel helped John

Cusack's Lloyd Dobler—and so many other men around the world—woo the girl.

And when the plane took off in the last scene and the fictional couple held hands, you asked, "Would you hold my hand like that next time we're on a plane?" Of course I said yes.

"I wish we could stay on the phone even while we slept tonight, but that would destroy my phone bill," you said. "But let's listen to this song until the end of the credits."

We listened and watched until our TVs went black. "Good night," we said at the same time.

...

We didn't mention marriage—the word or the concept. It felt like poison to us. We didn't want to stick our feet in its drying cement. We felt like we knew better.

We heard opinions from people who were husbands, wives, "partners," people in "complicated" relationships, as well as those who were perpetually or newly single.

*Just pretend it's a paper that says you can share insurance*, our married friends said.

*Stay strong*, said our divorced friends.

"Let's take our time," I told you. You nodded, glad for my caution. I think we both knew that the word *time* in that statement didn't have any real meaning.

...

Sometimes I remember something strange and seemingly un-important like the taste of a barbecue chicken sandwich or a friend's dog's name. It always seems to happen in the exact same spot where I remembered something last time. As if that specific part of the Burnside Bridge or the escalator at Pioneer Place is some kind of time/memory portal.

Sometimes I think I'll remember something forever and I forget it two months later, while smaller, more trivial moments stick with me for years. For instance, I have a hard time recalling exactly where we went out to breakfast after our first night together, but I can never forget when your dad gave us a jigsaw puzzle for Christmas.

One night, after some drinks, and after the kids went to bed, you took a Xanax and said to me, "Let's neck." And then we hooked our necks like swans. I completely forgot about that until just now.

. . .

You told me that your skin gets darker in the sun. "I'm going to get darker this summer. Just you watch," you said.

And I did watch.

Like when I was a kid I would sometimes stare at the clock to see if I could see the time moving. The minute hand and its slow crawl.

I think about your skin and how it tans so nice and gold-en. I want to watch the color changing, up and down your arms and legs, like a slowed-down magic trick.

...

We snuck into the pool at the apartments down the street. You looked amazing in your vintage bikini. I was pasty and white compared to the few other people lounging around the poolside. They eyed us suspiciously. I wanted to impress you by swimming a couple of laps, but I was winded within seconds.

"When was the last time you went swimming?" you asked me from the shallow end.

I had to catch my breath before saying, "I can't remember."

You dog-paddled to me and then slipped under the water and put your hand up like a shark fin. When you came back up, your whole body was shining, every bead of water like a stolen diamond.

...

Sometimes you have a hard time showing me your body. When we go to bed, you turn off the light before taking your clothes off. By the time my eyes adjust to see anything, you're already under the covers with me.

"I want to see you," I say.

"You can feel me," you say.

"But I like looking at you," I say.

"Why do men always have to be so visual?" you say. I'm not sure if you're exasperated or inquisitive.

"I want you to please all my senses," I say.

"But what if I don't?" you say.

...

"You're like a sexual predator," you said. "The way you walk, the way you breathe."

I wanted to ask *why, when, where.*

"The way you look at me feels like an attack," you said.

I said nothing but couldn't help thinking, *Get her. Get her. Attack!*

...

One night I pretended to die while we had sex. I clutched my heart and you laughed. You knew I was faking it because I cracked a smile. I lay still under you, staring blankly at the ceiling to the right of your head, your blurry, bobbing hair. Dark lightbulb. You slowed down and then started to cry. Sometimes you cry when you come. I wasn't sure what kind of tears they were. Maybe tears of pleasure, or frustration, or sadness. I thought maybe you were faking it.

When you were done, I stayed flat and lifeless, trying not to blink. You got out of bed and delicately pulled the blanket up to cover my body. You draped it over my face. My still feet sticking out.

...

I used to drive by my old girlfriends' places and try to catch glimpses of them. I'm still friends with a few and could have called them on the phone for a nice conversation, but that seemed too rehearsed or staged or something. I liked the possibility of seeing something more random from them. I imagined what they were like with their guards down.

I didn't tell you about this because you might not have understood it and I wasn't sure if I could explain.

Some of the things I noticed on these drive-bys:

Mimi likes to sit in her front yard and read on a beach towel, flexing her toes in the air every time she turns a page. Diane leaves her shades open all the time, sometimes paying bills at her dining room table or talking on the phone. Annette is always on the couch with her new husband, the TV light flickering on her face.

I drove by slowly, sometimes parked for a while, and wondered if I'd had any effect on them and if I somehow haunted them. I wondered how people carry on.

I did this with you too, but you didn't know it. It was before we lived together, whenever we got into fights. But I could only see your faint shadow in the window, maybe pacing or dancing with Maxine. I wanted to park my car, walk up closer, and peep between the curtains. I stayed in the car, though. If I rolled the windows down, I thought I'd be able to hear something, smell something, or feel some little clue in the air between us.

...

Sometimes you got long letters from your aunt Lydia in Missouri. After your mom died, she tried to become a surrogate mom for you. You were twenty-two years old at the time and your conservative aunt just annoyed you, for the most part.

But eventually you started to like her a little and use her as a long-distance confidante. A couple of times a year, you'd get a bulky nine-by-twelve envelope in the mail from her. It would include photographs, clippings of uptight advice columns and op-eds, and a letter of at least twenty pages. Sometimes there was also a fifty-dollar bill, folded up and concealed inside a Doublemint gum wrapper. Aunt Lydia did not have email because she said the government controls it.

You did your best to write a long reply back to her, sometimes taking a couple of months to do so. You also included various news clippings and photographs, but no cash.

You locked yourself in the bathroom one night, rereading a new letter and replying to her. You came out once and asked me impatiently to look up a word in the dictionary for you.

"What is it?" I asked.

"Rancor," you said.

I'd heard the word before but was not sure what it meant. I thumbed through our paperback dictionary. "It says: *Bitter, long-lasting resentment.*" I closed the book and looked up. You were back in the bathroom already. "Wait a second," I said. "Use it in a sentence."

You didn't reply.

"Why do you need to know that word?" I asked through the door.

"Oh, nothing," you said.

"Are you okay in there?"

"Almost done!"

"Tell Lydia I said hello."

No response.

"Can I go to the bathroom?"
"No."

...

It took Vince a while to outgrow his wizard phase. He read about them constantly for almost five years and had wizard-themed birthday parties for three years in a row. He started dressing like a wizard too. He even got Maxine to play along. Sometimes we saw them, dressed in capes and odd pointy hats, walking around the neighborhood. They would go to the big grocery store up the street and look at the mass-market books about magical demons and other ridiculous creatures.

One day I saw Maxine putting eyeliner on Vince and then they followed me around the apartment for several hours, asking if they could hypnotize me. I didn't know if they wanted to look into my past or glimpse the future. I finally let them do it and I actually fell asleep.

When I woke up, they looked scared and then avoided me for the rest of the weekend.

...

There was a big rainstorm and our electricity was out all night. We all walked around with flashlights in our hands. Vince had a toy hard hat from when he was five with a light attached to it, like a miner's. He squeezed it onto his eleven-year-old head.

For dinner we ate salad, with candles lighting the table. After that, we made up a game called Darkness Monster, which was basically hide-and-seek in the dark with flashlights. It turned out to be a really fun game until Maxine stubbed her toe on the couch.

After we put the kids to bed, we found our old alarm clocks and wound them up and put them on our bedside table (we had to wake up at 7:00 AM for school). I tried to read with Vince's hard hat on my head but it kept falling off and then its light burned out. You were using your flashlight to make animal shadows on the wall. "Let me see your hand," you said. You tried to incorporate it into something you were doing, an elephant or some kind of bird. The way you were touching my hand got me excited. You shined your flashlight on the bulge in my shorts and then scooted down. "Let's see what this can turn into," you said. You slipped my shorts off and put the flashlight up close to my cock. You circled it with the beam, like a helicopter light looking for a criminal on the run. The room was totally dark except my cock in the spotlight. Then I saw half of your face enter the light and the cock disappeared. I grabbed the flashlight and angled it so that I could see the new shadows you were making with me.

. . .

There was a time when you didn't want to have oral sex. You said it was a rape scene in a recent movie that was traumatizing you.

"It's just a movie," I said.

"But it happens," you said. "It almost happened to me. I mean, it did sort of happen to me. I don't ever talk about it."

"When?" I said. "I didn't know."

"I was fourteen. At music camp. I'm only going to tell you this story once."

"Go ahead," I said. "It's okay."

"It was such a gross place. I was one of the youngest people there and everyone was cracking dirty jokes all the time. Everyone seemed delinquent. There was a break every day that lasted two hours and kids would run off and make out. It was at this big high school in St. Louis. There was a classroom that someone found unlocked, so they called it the mashroom. Guys would tell you to meet them in the mashroom. You could say no if you wanted to but then they'd be really mean to you."

I watched your eyes to gauge the pain of the memories, but at the same time my mind was racing forward on its own, filling in blanks. I felt perverse. I looked down at your hands holding each other.

"I went to the mashroom once, with my friend Susan Pelt. We were going to spy but the door was closed. So we went outside and looked through the window. We saw a girl named Krystal in there with an older boy. They were sort of on top of the teacher's desk. We heard some muffled sounds but I couldn't tell what they were doing. She was wearing a shirt that was unbuttoned most of the way and the boy looked like he was squeezing her too hard and sort of humping against her legs. I could see one of her nipples and I stared really hard, trying to get a good look at it because I hadn't seen another girl's nipple before. Susan nudged me and said, 'Maybe we should help her,' and I looked at her and almost laughed. And then when I looked back, Krystal was sitting up on the desk and buttoning up her shirt. Susan ran away from the window but I wanted to stay and see who was next in the mashroom. But the boy wouldn't let Krystal leave. He was standing in front of the door and whispering something urgent. He unzipped his pants and I saw his dick. I remember thinking it looked like a finger."

You held your hand in front of your face, as if to see what fingers really looked like. Your eyes squinted and then you looked back to me. Instead of smirking or letting out a laugh, you exhaled audibly through your nose.

"He sort of nodded down at it," you continued. "And I watched her bend down and kiss it right on the head. He put his own hand on it then and it grew bigger. *His fingers around the finger*, I thought, and that kept scrolling through my mind. Fingers around the finger . . . a six-fingered hand . . . Krystal watched it and looked worried. He would stop and nod and she bent down and kissed it but I could tell that he wasn't satisfied. He pushed her awkwardly to one knee. Then she looked around and got on both knees. I decided I wanted Susan to save her then, to come bursting through the door. I could have thrown something through the window but I didn't want to get caught. He put one of his fingers in her mouth and then another, and then he grabbed her hand and put her fingers in his own mouth, like he was showing her. Like he was sharing something."

I was relieved that it wasn't you that this happened to, but I still tasted a sick kind of sour rise into my throat. My mind made this story into a movie and you were the director. That window was the camera that you hid behind. But your memory is the film still looped inside you.

...

One night while drinking, we pretended that we had forgotten how to kiss. We pushed and slid our slack, unpuckered lips on each other's faces, our mouths like half-dead people in a vast desert. In a way, it was exciting and new. In a way, it was almost innocent. It was almost funny. We almost started laughing.

...

Our friend James has some kind of muscular dystrophy and has to use a wheelchair when it's really bad. It started to affect him when he was in his twenties. He was always shy around girls even though he's a decent-looking guy. When he first met you, he had a hard time talking to you too. But recently, it seems like he has a new girlfriend every other month, and they're each more beautiful than the last. We wonder how he does it but we don't say anything to him because we can't figure out how to phrase the question.

I'm trying to figure out how much of it is sympathy and how much of it is something else.

"It's a nursing fantasy," you told me once. "Some women like to take care of someone who needs help. It gives them a sense of purpose."

"Do you have a nursing fantasy?" I asked you. It felt weird to say *nursing*, like I was talking about breast-feeding.

"Not yet," you said. "We'll see how your health stands up though."

"Would you like it if I were a male nurse?" I asked you.

You laughed but didn't say anything. I imagined you in a wheelchair and me in some male nurse-type clothes. A light-blue V-neck shirt and paper-thin pants.

I wanted to tell you about a cute girl in a wheelchair I'd seen at the grocery store the other day. She was being pushed around by a guy and I was sort of envious of him. Her hands looked pretty and still in her lap. I decided not to mention this girl.

We saw James a few days after this conversation and he was with a high-heeled Puerto Rican who looked like Miss Universe. We were at a restaurant, and when he had to use the bathroom, she went with him and I became almost outraged with jealousy. I realized that he must have figured something out about women, maybe tapped into some psychological perspective that helped his confidence.

After dinner, we all left the restaurant and I asked James and his new woman if they wanted to catch a cab with us, but they said they were only going a few blocks and it was downhill. She started to push his wheelchair but he stopped her and said, "Let me give you a ride." She smiled and then sat sweetly in his lap. He pushed his wheels forward and they began gliding like magic.

I looked at you and said the same words: "Let me give *you* a ride." You jumped on my back and off we went.

...

We had two lists of dreams written out. We hung them in the bathroom for laughs. There were age-appropriate dreams and infinite dreams.

On the age-appropriate list were things like: start a band together and call it Year of Slacks, go to the Rock and Roll Hall of Fame in Cleveland, get and maintain a flat stomach, and win a dance contest.

On the list of infinite dreams: write some poems together, go to Paris, buy a nice watch, and make enough money so we can learn to play golf.

Our friends asked us about the lists sometimes. They wanted to know why they were in the bathroom. That's the room where most of the aging happens, we said.

...

I sometimes wonder if you've ever thought about hiring a seductress to test me. Maybe a friend of yours I haven't met before, or a stranger.

Would she come to my work and start hitting on me? Slip me her phone number with a wink? I would get suspicious if that happened.

Or maybe when I go to the grocery store, you call the secret seducer and tell her what store I'm going to. What happens next—does she dress up sexy and find me in the cat food aisle? Does she ask my opinion on the organic beef and make a bad joke about how much she loves meat?

That might actually work.

Is there a website where you can find people who test the will of your husband, wife, or lover? I imagine a logo with an apple, a snake, and naked cartoon bodies trying to hide their guilt.

You once said, "There's no such thing as entrapment when loved ones are involved." At least I think I've heard you say that before.

Sometimes, late at night, we find ourselves watching a reality TV show in which unfaithful people are secretly followed and filmed. They are seen with their lovers eating at places like Olive Garden or some bar in the next town over. We hear them talking on their bugged cell phones, telling their waiting loved ones that they have too much work to do or will be out late with "friends." They drive to cheap hotels and then we watch the minutes lapse away on the corner of the screen. When they are done, they come back outside and then the host of the show exits his surveillance van and jogs with a cameraman and the betrayed lover across a parking lot. We watch through the eyes of the shaky handheld camera as it readies its attack. There is a stunned pause and then an ugly confrontation.

I sometimes imagine that it's us on the screen because I know you fantasize about this too.

...

I found a couple of journals of yours and they were full of peppy inspirational sayings right alongside depressing entries about how you see yourself. It didn't seem like you at all but I knew it was you because of the handwriting. If I had found the journals somewhere, like on a bus, and they were written by someone else, I would have shown them to you and we'd likely make fun of them.

I read bits of the journals when I found them mixed into a box of old fashion magazines. I felt a little uncomfortable, so I put them back. That night I asked you slyly about how long you'd been keeping journals and you said that you'd started when you were a junior in high school. You told me that there were possibly twenty or thirty journals stored away in a box somewhere, but you never looked at them. "It's like when people want to be frozen and brought back to life later," you said. "I've frozen parts of my youth."

I didn't tell you about the ones I'd found. One was pretty recent, from when we first started dating. There were a lot of entries about your job at the library. Wonderfully fantastic daydreams mixed with complaints about coworkers. Many of the entries were more neurotic and adult, as opposed to the trivial and childish thoughts of a teenage diary.

"Do you want those years of your youth brought back to life?" I asked you.

"I should burn them," you said with a laugh.

The rest of that week, I found myself drawn to that more recent journal. I tried to keep it in a secret place in the bedroom, where I could get it out and read it whenever I had time. There were a few parts where you expressed uncertainty about me. You wrote a couple of things about me that weren't totally accurate, and I wanted to cross them out and correct them. Or maybe just smudge them a little so you couldn't read them. One of the things you wrote was that I am too eager a lover. A couple of weeks after that, you wrote that I seemed nervous around Maxine and I might not be the best father figure for her.

My questions at dinner probably seemed strange that week. "Do you think I've become a better lover than I was at the beginning?"

You answered this question as I had hoped. "Yes, of course. I think you used to be kind of eager, but it's very beautiful and natural now. We've learned each other's bodies." Your answer was sweet and reassuring, but the word *eager* jumped out at me most of all. It was like some secret hunchback who lived in the basement, who had always wanted to meet me and pat my back in a condescending manner. "Congratulations," it might slobber. "You are not eager anymore."

"Do you think I'm becoming a good father figure for Maxine?" I asked the next night.

"Maxine looks up to you," you said. "She knows you more now and she trusts you. She loves you because she knows I love you."

A couple of days after that, the journal seemed to disappear. But I was glad to be free of it. I felt like my questions were getting annoying for you anyway, especially the desperate way I asked them, like a man trying to erase your memory of his past behavior. I was bringing my eager and nervous self back to life. I had thawed it out until it was finally ready to burn.

. . .

We were lying on the bed naked and you apologized about your pubic hair. "I keep forgetting to trim it," you said. And then you handed me a pair of scissors.

I scooted down and started running my fingers through it. "I like it this way," I said, and formed a Mohawk shape.

"Feel free to do whatever," you said.

I started trimming it down a little. I blew the tiny blonde specks of hair onto your belly. I made a face with them and then a circle. Then I slowly ushered them into your belly button like I was filling a hole.

. . .

You told me I was talking in my sleep and I wasn't sure I believed you.

"Most of it was just random shouting," you said. "And then you just laughed this really fucked-up laugh."

"You don't remember what I was shouting?"

"You said, 'Don't touch that. Keep it over there!' And I asked you what not to touch and you just grumbled."

I thought about this for a while and started to remember the dream. I was supposed to be guarding a giant sex toy. Some man had brought it into a McDonald's and then asked me to watch it while he went to the bathroom. I was sitting at the table next to his eating an endless box of Chicken McNuggets. I told the man, who was old and hunched, that I would watch his toy. It looked like a dildo but there was something else attached to it. A circle of feathers and a metal thing that looked like a fingernail clipper. The man was in the bathroom for a long time and people kept walking over to look at the thing, so I kept telling people to get away. In the dream, I was using very colorful language. Riffing wildly like a stand-up comedian. The man finally came out and walked over to his table and said *thanks*. Then he picked up his hamburger and walked out without his sex toy. I didn't stop him or call out to him. And then I thought I could make a lot of money on the sex toy, so I grabbed it off the table and ran out of there with it. A couple of people started chasing me but they were really small, like kids, and it was easy for me to break their tackles. I was like Barry Sanders or Adrian Peterson, knocking people over, juking them out of their shoes, or stiff-arming them. I knew the sex toy was mine and as soon as I got it to a pawn shop, I'd be rolling in the dough. That's why I was laughing.

But for some reason, I was a little disturbed by the sex toy, so instead I told you it was a golden box full of diamonds and heroin.

"Your subconscious must be pretty active," you said. "I hope you got some good money for it."

"Yeah, I don't think I actually made it to the pawn shop," I said.

"That's what you get for eating Chicken McNuggets," you said.

...

You told me about the time you broke your hymen when you were thirteen. You were on a camping trip with your family and you were all on a horseback tour around some mountain in the Ozarks. It was you, your mom and dad, your brother, and a guide who called himself "Shoe." He pointed at the horse and said, "Horse." And then he pointed at himself and said, "Shoe." It was the only funny thing that he said. The rest of the time, you said, he talked about this plant and that trail and Lewis and Clark and stuff you didn't care about.

It was your first time on a horse and his name was Thunder. He was the color of cotton balls and his back was just a couple of inches taller than your head. You were so excited about this day and had thought about it ever since school had gotten out for the summer.

Toward the end of the tour, Shoe was leading your family along a stream when his horse suddenly reared up and backed into your dad's. Then your dad's horse backed into your mom's and hers backed up into yours. It was a big rattlesnake that had spooked them. Thunder darted away from the pack and you lunged forward, holding on to the rope but also to the horse's mane. The saddle slipped and you felt the hard leather horn push between your legs. Shoe steered his horse over to you and settled Thunder down. You were crying and felt paralyzed by fear. You didn't want to look down. You remembered your mom said, "Oh, my baby." Your brother tried not to laugh but his mouth shaped into a smirk.

When all of you were returning to the horses' ranch, you saw another family waiting their turn. A big family, mostly teenagers it seemed. Like ten of them, you said. At first they were smiling and then their faces changed. They were all looking at you. Instinctively you lowered your head. Then you saw what they saw: the blood on the saddle and down your legs.

You wanted to ride off and disappear, you said. You wanted to stay on the horse until everything was back to normal.

...

I think I may have lost my virginity to my cousin/babysitter but I'm not totally sure. She was with me one night when I was twelve and my parents were out playing poker somewhere. She was seventeen and her name was Wendy. I remember she was trying to teach me how to play a card game and then I was suddenly ill and feeling woozy like I had food poisoning or had been drugged. I passed out for a while and when I woke up, Wendy was taking a shower. I was on the couch and she came out in a towel. Maybe it was the wet blonde hair or maybe it was the sight of her smooth tan legs and bare feet, but I suddenly thought she was the most alluring and beautiful girl I had ever laid eyes on. She sat next to me and then started crying and saying she was sorry. Her eyes were closed and it looked like she might have been in some kind of dream state. But I noticed that I felt better than before. I also noticed I had an erection.

"I think I did something bad," Wendy kept saying.

I didn't know how to respond and I said quietly, "What did you do? What did you do?"

She opened her eyes and looked at me and asked, "How do you feel? Are you all right?"

"I feel good," I said. "I'm having fun."

That was the last time I saw Wendy. My parents never mentioned her again, but I thought about her for a long time.

...

When I was eighteen, I started to like another girl named Wendy. She was also blonde and sat in front of me in two classes. She was maybe a little taller than I was and ran track and field. She was going out with a friend of mine named Derrick, but I heard that she had other boyfriends at other schools. She seemed dangerous somehow. I spent a lot of time staring at the back of her head and hoping for a breeze to blow her scent back to me.

One night, I was at my first party where there were no adults anywhere. People were making out everywhere, like they'd never have a chance to make out again. I saw Wendy and Derrick but there was something tense going on between them. He was really drunk and couldn't stand up straight. I helped Wendy prop him up on a big old couch that looked like it would be hard to get up from. Then Wendy asked me to drive her to another house.

I didn't have my own car yet but I drove my mom's Pontiac sometimes. It didn't even have a cassette player. Wendy pulled out a mixtape and looked around the dashboard for somewhere to insert it. "I just have a radio," I said.

"I see that," she said. She pushed the tape back into her bag.

When we got to the other house, I wasn't sure who lived there but it looked like another party. Wendy asked me to wait a couple of minutes and then ran inside. I wasn't sure what she was doing in there but she came back after four or five songs and some commercials had played on the radio.

"Do you want to go back now?" I asked her.

"I don't think so," she said, and scooted closer to me.

The front and back seats of the Pontiac were like long vinyl couches.

We started kissing and she leaned back, pulling me on top of her. Besides possibly that hazy night with my cousin Wendy, I hadn't had sex yet but it seemed like it was about to happen. I was trying to slow it down, trying to ask her about Derrick or whose house we were parked in front of, but she pushed her mouth harder on mine and I gave up after a while. We took off our pants but kept our shirts and coats on. She said, "Don't worry. I'm on the pill." We fogged up the cold windows.

There didn't seem to be a need to talk after we were through, and I drove her back to the first party, where Derrick was passed out on the couch where we'd left him. I felt embarrassed for some reason and wanted to talk to her about what had happened but didn't know how to. She went off with one of her girlfriends and I got back in the Pontiac alone.

I still stared at the back of her head the rest of the year, but that's as far as I got.

. . .

You told me that when you had your first high school boyfriend, you used to go to his house after school and put your head on his stomach. He was a big guy. Sumo wrestler legs, broad shoulders, and round beer belly, even though he was too young to drink beer. You said his belly was like a pillow, and when you heard it grumble it turned you on. Sometimes it became a game. You wouldn't have sex with him until he was "hungry for it."

I imagined your ear on him and the sounds his body would make. "What did it sound like?" I asked you.

"Like a lion, drowning in an ocean," you said.

. . .

We once decided that we would surprise Vince and Maxine by getting them a dog. We went to the pound and found one we liked, a two-year-old medium springer spaniel with white and caramel-brown hair.

We took him home and the kids became very excited when we walked in carrying the shy dog. Maxine wanted to play catch with him, but the dog was young and untrained. Vince wanted to wrestle with him. We took photos of the kids with the dog, and I told them about how I took pictures of my dog when I was a boy, and I could see how much the dog (and even I) grew. I still have those Polaroids with the dates penciled in on the bottom.

In the morning though, Vince was stuffed up and his face was puffy. We realized that he was allergic to the dog's hair. We had to take the dog back.

There have been a few times since that day when the kids have seen those photos in our coffee-table photo album and wondered out loud about what happened to the dog. I should just take them out. It's probably best that they forget that day, and the gift we had to take away from them before they got attached.

. . .

We showed Vince and Maxine how to press aluminum foil against their faces to make robot masks. They punched out holes for their eyes and wore wraparound sunglasses. We took out the video camera and decided to create a robot talk show. We interviewed the kids like they were movie stars. Then we made dinner, moving around the kitchen like robots. Then we made signs that said FREE THE ROBOTS and told the kids to walk around the neighborhood with them. When they came back, they asked if we could make this Robot Day. We said sure, we could make it an annual event. But for some reason, we never celebrated Robot Day again.

. . .

Sometimes your mood was unsettled and volatile. The kids noticed this, and then our home felt tense and they'd get quiet. It was up to me to open you up and help you feel better somehow. This was usually done through a series of earnest questions, half jokes, apologies, and lofty promises.

But sometimes it was me who was in a bad mood or feeling hopeless, and you weren't sure how to change that. You'd say, "I'm the one who gets depressed, not you."

If we were depressed at the same time, it felt like no one could help us, not even the kids. We'd send them off to a friend or relative's house. And then you'd start slugging me in the arm. "You can't be depressed when I'm depressed. I need you to be the level-headed one."

"Why can't you be the level-headed one?" I asked. "I need you to do that for me sometimes, you know?"

Your slugs were harmless at first but they got harder. When the bruise appeared, you'd cry and rub your face on it.

. . .

Sometimes I wanted to unload some anger, even just once, to see what you'd do. I wanted to stop you and say "fuck off" to your face and see how deeply you could be hurt. It would be easier than saying "I hate you." I often wondered if "I hate you" would be the same thing as "I don't love you."

. . .

I'd rather have a tomboy for a girlfriend than someone who always fussed about makeup and expensive fashion. I got turned on when you talked about football with me.

But I still liked high heels and your delicate hairstyles that no one was allowed to touch.

And I liked you in that black dress that showed your back.

That part of your collarbone that I could scoop sugar out of.

Lips swelling red.

I took a snapshot of this version of you in my mind—a sort of high-maintenance bitch. I savored this side of you. The prim and perfect woman who secretly wanted to be torn apart. You always gave me something to look forward to.

. . .

I slapped you lightly when you said you liked it rough. You laughed, so I slapped you harder. I called your pussy a "thirty-five-year-old pussy." But you pinched my face like a weird grandmother.

...

About a year after we moved in together, you showed me a police report about an ex-boyfriend. He had physically abused you for most of your eight-month relationship. It was a three-page list of dates from about twelve years before, with descriptions like: *February 12: Defendant accused claimant of flirting with his friends and slapped claimant at public café. When claimant tried to calm defendant down, defendant yelled at her and pushed her as he exited café.*

There were about thirty incidents listed, and at first I couldn't believe all of these things had happened to you. You had never mentioned this relationship before. It took me a moment to fathom what I was looking at. The first thing I asked you was why you had stayed in the relationship.

"I had a really dear boyfriend who had just moved away and I was really vulnerable."

Before I got a chance to read more, you grabbed the papers from my hands and put them away. I didn't get to see what the guy's name was and you wouldn't tell me. "He's still in the music scene here, so I can't really talk about it. I got a restraining order and he'll go to jail if he's anywhere near me."

I felt shocked and my face went white as I looked at you.

"I didn't know if I could ever mention it," you said. "It's not like I can just insert into the conversation: *Did I ever tell you about the boyfriend who beat me up for eight months?*"

An hour earlier, we had been having sex and playfully acting rough with each other. You bit me and then I pretended to slap you and hold you down. Now I suddenly felt guilty and overwhelmed and started crying. You put your arms around me and my face rested between your breasts. "I hope I didn't remind you of him," I said.

"You never remind me of anyone," you said. "You just remind me of love."

. . .

Vince told me he had been planning to go to a movie with his friend Tyler, but then his new friend Alex wanted to go skateboarding instead. He hung out with Tyler on most Saturdays, sometimes reluctantly, so I thought it would be fine if he did something with Alex for a change. I wasn't really sure if I liked Tyler much anyhow.

I heard Vince telling Tyler on the phone that I wouldn't let him go out because he got a bad grade on a math test. I didn't approve of this lie but I understood it. I didn't say anything to Vince about it. An hour later, Alex came over and they headed out on their skateboards.

While you and I were eating lunch that afternoon, Tyler called and asked if he could talk to Vince. My stomach tied itself into a knot and I told him that Vince was grounded for the day. I said something about the math test. At first, Tyler sounded suspicious, and then his voice sounded heavy and wounded. "I was in the car with my mom and I thought I saw him at Alberta Park," he said.

I felt my throat get dry. "If he was at the park, he wasn't supposed to be," I said.

There was an impatient silence coming from Tyler's side

of the phone line. I felt a little bad that Vince's lie, probably one of his first ones of betrayal, wasn't quite foolproof. Maybe he hadn't thought it through well enough. He still had some work to do before he was as good a liar as I was.

I got off the phone and sat there for a moment, thinking about what to do. I wondered if Tyler would get on his bike and go back to Alberta Park to see if it was Vince. I knew he probably would. You noticed me thinking deeply about this and asked me what was wrong, but I didn't want to say anything to implicate Vince.

My heart beat fast as I drove to Alberta Park. I wanted to make sure Vince's lie was safe. Sometimes the truth can be harmless, but it can feel bad to the person on the short end of it.

. . .

I was driving on the freeway one morning when someone cut in front of me with his BMW. I honked my horn but the guy seemed oblivious and uncaring. I sped up and tailgated him. I've always had a fantasy about ramming my car into the back bumper of a shitty driver, just to scare him. I was accelerating so much this time that I almost did it for real. The BMW took the next exit and I jerked to the left at the last second to stay on the freeway. But I was going so fast that I lost control of the car and stomped on the brakes. I spun a blurry circle toward the side of the road, and for a moment it felt as if my tires had lifted off the ground. Somehow I ended up not hitting any other cars and barely missed T-boning myself on the V of the exit ramp. My car stopped on the shoulder of the exit, and I thought for sure that the driver's side would be scraped all to hell by the rail I was up against. An old man pulled over to check and see if I was okay. My car was facing the wrong way, so we were looking at each other, face to face through our windshields. I rolled my window down and yelled out that I was fine. I motioned him to go around as I maneuvered my car so I could get out and inspect the damage. I was shaking as I got out of the car but then relieved to see that there was no damage at all. I was surprised by this and by the fact that I hadn't even blown a tire in the skid.

I saw some friends an hour later and told them about what had happened. My body was still vibrating from it and my brain kept telling me how lucky I was. It kept saying, "You could be in the hospital right now. You could be dying right now."

When I saw you later, right before dinner, you told me about all the things you did during the day and the plans you had for the next day. You talked without giving me a chance to answer. You were hyper and full of energy. I tried to find a moment to tell you about the accident but it started to feel less urgent. I made the mistake of telling you other trivial things first—our friend's new dog, the movie I wanted to see, what we needed at the store. By then it was too late.

I decided I wouldn't tell you. It would be another secret, thrown on the pile with the others. And I sometimes think of it that way—a smelly little stack of hidden things festering somewhere. I rummage through it with my hands, holding up older secrets and trying to figure out what they are exactly. Some so moldy, dusty, and threadbare that they're like old clothes decomposed on a corpse.

"What's wrong?" you asked me. And that was my opening, my chance to tell.

"Nothing," I said. I liked saying that word sometimes, so I said it again. You smiled, knowing nothing was wrong.

. . .

You told me you had a surprise and asked me to wait in the bedroom for you. You told me to take off my clothes and then dimmed the lights until you were almost shadow. You told me to close my eyes and I did.

I heard you doing something by the closet. Buttoning up, unsnapping, or maybe tying something. Music came on— piano and words of longing. I started to feel some kind of pressure to act surprised when I opened my eyes. Or maybe it wasn't surprise that you were preparing for me. I was probably thinking too much about it. I suddenly felt vulnerable in my nudity.

Then I felt your hands cup my face and you whispered, "Hi there." I opened my eyes and looked at you, my eyes adjusting to the near dark. "Do you like it?" you asked. You were wearing a tight black nightie and a dark wig. Instead of the best simple answer ("yes"), I tried to admire the style, the softness of the fabric. Maybe it was something fancier than a nightie. I was struck with uncertainty.

I said, "What is it?"

You snapped upright and scowled. "Forget it," you said, flicking the music off.

"Well, no," I said. "I just can't really see it."

"It's stupid," you said.

"No, it's good," I said quickly. "Let me get a better look."

"You're not supposed to ask me what it is," you said. "You're just supposed to tear it off. Never mind." You grabbed some clothes and left the room. "I need to get out of here."

I stayed on the bed, naked and stunned. It was after midnight but I wasn't tired. I looked at my penis like it was to blame, or like it could have saved me. I stared at it as time passed. I grabbed it and looked at it from all different angles. I wanted to find a mirror and look at it a new way, like that movie where the women looked at their vaginas and felt empowered.

My phone buzzed on the dresser, startling me. You were calling. I let it ring eight times and then answered cautiously.

"Hey, baby! Guess what! Guess what!" you said, getting louder with each word. I wondered if you were already drunk. I thought you were doing that trick where you do the nice exclamation before the mad exclamation.

"What now?" I said. I instantly felt bad for saying *now*, but you didn't seem to notice.

"I found a fifty-dollar bill! Fifty bucks!"

"Oh," I said. "That's nice."

"Come down here and have a drink with me," you said. "I'll give you money for the jukebox. We'll play pool too!"

I got dressed and walked down to the bar.

When I got there, you had our drinks side by side and the pool balls racked up. Your black wig was still on and you strutted around the table, air-guitaring your pool stick. You smiled like a sneaky criminal. It was like the nightie thing hadn't happened. But then your smile turned dark and you said, "I'm gonna beat you real bad tonight."

# YEAR THREE

You kicked me out of the apartment for the afternoon and told me to call you when I felt scared about something. "You're so calm," you told me. "I want to hear what you'd sound like when you're in distress."

I went down to the boxing club that we always drove by on our way home from Saturday breakfast. There were big windows all around the place, and I watched two sweaty men going full throttle on each other in one of the boxing rings. They looked like chiseled boulders with tattoos. One of them landed four alternating punches to the other's ribs. *Left right left right.* I imagined my ribs getting punched like that. Four blows in one excruciating second. I felt my ribs buckle, the bones caving in and stabbing my lungs. The winning fighter took a wide swing at the other's head—a fast and vicious-looking roundhouse. The losing fighter was wearing some kind of headgear, but it looked loose. A red mouthpiece flew through the air and landed, sliding across the ring.

I thought to myself: *The fighter is going to spit now. Maybe a string of blood or a tooth.* But I wondered if they were supposed to spit. *If my mouth was ever full of my own blood, should I spit or should I swallow? What if the beating continued?*

I walked down the street and found a quiet place to call you. An alleyway. When you answered the phone, I started screaming like I was being beaten, like I needed you to call 911. But I wasn't saying words. I was just shouting in a way that seemed to say, *Hurry up! This is the end. Hurry up—I am going to die!*

I hung up the phone and started to walk home.

Twenty minutes later, you called me and started screaming too. It was a horrible sound. The sound of fear and violence. It was guttural and ugly. But then you were suddenly laughing. A giggle that turned into a cackle. It sounded like you were out of breath and wheezing. "Wait. Let me try that again," you said. You hung up and called me back, screaming again.

...

We were sitting on a bench at the park when we noticed a girl jog by with her dog. The girl was short and punky, her skirt and leggings torn. Her makeup looked applied and then smeared. The dog was bigger than she was.

"Let's follow her," you said.

We walked quickly down the path and saw her come to a large fenced-in area. When we got to the fence, your face turned pale.

"Is this a dog park?" you asked me.

"Yeah. It's the biggest one in the city," I told you. I thought maybe you were afraid of big dogs. "What's wrong?"

"My mom told me about this place. She made me promise that I would come down here and look at it before she died, and I never did."

"Did your mom have a dog?" I watched your eyes become wet.

"No. I think she just wanted me to see something alive."

"Is this okay?" I asked. "Do you want to leave?"

You didn't say anything. We stood there and watched all the dogs. There were about twenty dogs in there. It was the middle of the day. The owners stood around the periphery, like parents watching their kids play. A couple of dogs were playing rough and growling and nipping each other. "Hey! Hey!" the dog owners would sometimes chide.

The girl with the big dog stood in the far corner. Her dog seemed unexcited by it all. It sat at her feet and watched us watching the dogs. After a few minutes, you noticed the punk girl and her dog watching us. You smiled and nudged me with your elbow. "There she is," you said.

. . .

You told me never to worry about you. You ate tuna from the can. I thought about knocking it out of your hand, but which direction? Straight down, so it would splat on the floor? Underhand, so it would enter your eyes? It's not you I worry about.

. . .

One morning, I had sex with you but then felt like masturbating just a few hours later. I was at work so I couldn't.

On my lunch break, I was propositioned by a stranger in the parking garage. He was wearing a helmet—one of those bike helmets that look like a turtle shell. "Can I give you a ride? I have protection," he said. He showed me his bike, held his hand out and gave it a flourish, like, *Isn't it a nice machine?* I told him thank you and held my hand out to him, mostly out of curiosity.

I still felt unsatisfied that night, but I also felt normal. I wanted to tell you about all of this, but I didn't think I would have the tightest answers to the loosest questions you'd ask. For instance: *Why?*

...

"Love doesn't just fall out of the sky," you said once. We were listening to a show on talk radio. You were scoffing at the host, who was offering hope to a heartbroken caller. Sometimes you talked back to radios, TVs, and real people.

"Let me cut through the bullshit of this dude's advice," you said to me. "People don't end up with people better than they are. It's always an equal pairing. Drug addicts end up with drug addicts. Fat people end up with fat people. Perverts end up with perverts. Boring people end up with boring people. If you're dating outside of your league, you're either one of the lucky few, or you're going to die a mysterious death in the wooded area behind your house."

"You should have your own show," I said, even though I

didn't really agree with your assessments.

"Damn right I should," you said.

We turned the radio off and drove in silence for a few minutes. "I love you," you finally said. We laughed so hard we nearly drove off the road.

...

Vince had his first babysitting job, watching a five-year-old next door for three hours. The mother gave him twenty dollars and I asked him what he was going to do with the money. He told me about some leather gloves that he wanted at the store down the street. It was nearly summer, too warm for gloves, so I asked him what he needed them for.

"I have a pair of gloves for yard work and a pair for snow," he said. "I think leather ones will be good social gloves."

I tried to think of what *social gloves* would be. I imagined Vince at a fancy dinner party, shaking hands with people. His hands would probably be uncomfortable and sweaty inside them, but his social gloves would be the talk of the room. I remembered certain things I wore as a kid to come across as more sophisticated or adult—my father's dress jackets, my first pair of slip-on shoes, and the fedora I took from my cousin's house without permission.

When Vince returned from the store, he did not have the gloves. "They were on sale this week and ran out," he said.

"It's probably too warm for them now anyway," I said. "Plus your hands are getting bigger. When it gets cold again, I'll buy you a pair and they'll fit better."

"My hands are getting bigger?" he said. He looked at his hands as if he hadn't ever thought about them before. "I guess you're right."

...

For the first couple of years, I was trying to learn as much as possible about you. I worried that your ex-husband knew more about you. I wanted all of his knowledge and more. He had to know that ants make you queasy, and he probably knew you didn't like talk shows.

Those things were easy to learn.

I wondered if he knew more intimate details than I did. Did you ever go through an anal phase? If so, when?

Did he know that thing I discovered about your chin and how it smells like white cheddar popcorn?

...

Sometimes I walked around with my cock sticking out of the front flap of my boxers, but only when it was erect. You were trying to check your email and I kept pacing closer to you. I started rubbing your back and you turned your head to put me in your mouth. My breath got quicker and you twisted in your chair for a better angle. I had to stand on the tips of my toes a little. I read through your email in-box while you sucked on me. Sarah, James, Jennifer, Dad, Chris, Sage, Rob, Rob, Rob, Sarah, Rob. I wondered why Rob emailed you so much. Was it the Rob from your library or some other Rob

I didn't know? Suddenly, the doorbell rang and you stopped. You shut down the computer and stood up. The doorbell rang again. "I owe you half a blow job," you said.

...

When we first met, I heard you talking to an old boyfriend on the phone and you were laughing a lot. I wasn't sure what was so funny, but I became surprisingly jealous. When you got off the phone, I said something about how I didn't like him and that you shouldn't be friends with him after the way he treated you. He was ten years older than you and also worked at the library. He read all the Russians, all the Eastern Europeans. You told me he "loathed" your American novels and self-help books. "You're letting him off the hook for all those times he talked down to you," I said.

"He only said those things because I went to a small college," you answered.

"He's a jerkhole," I said.

"Are you saying I can't be friends with him anymore?"

"I don't like the sound of your laugh with him," I said.

We were silent for a minute and you stared at me with hard, squinting eyes. "Is that going to be a rule?" you said.

"You can text him and you can email him, but no more talking," I said. I caught even myself off guard by how stern I was being, but in a strange way you seemed to like this punishment.

As far as I could tell, you obeyed this rigid rule. You earned some trust points, as our therapy-going friends called them. I wanted to lift the embargo on the phone calls with him, but

it was probably the only hard rule I had made in our relationship, and I shamefully liked that little sliver of power. It made
me feel manly, in an old-fashioned, patriarchal way.

I held on to that rule like a security blanket.

. . .

Sometimes we couldn't even be in the same room. Nothing
would be said directly about the tight knot of an argument
we'd had earlier. My behavior, you said, got me into situa-
tions with some of our female friends that felt too intimate. It
made me, and the people around me, vulnerable to bad deci-
sions, you told me. I didn't fully disagree with you, and that's
what made our simmering animosity linger for too long.

We were at home together, but we felt separate.

If one of us was sitting on the couch, the other was back in
the bedroom, writing emails, pillows propping us up. We might
come together in the kitchen after an hour or so. We each made
our own drinks and said something simple, like, "How are you
doing?" The answer was a shrug, or "I'm doing okay."

Then we'd switch places—me on the couch, you in the bedroom. You watching a movie on your laptop. Me reading with
the stereo on. I'd hear the bedroom door close. You didn't want
to hear my music. I didn't want to hear your movie.

It started to feel good, being apart like this and letting the
tension slowly dissipate. But the next day, even though it
would be small and hidden, it would still be there.

. . .

One time a friend of ours was over and you were getting pretty drunk with him. It was getting late and you told me to go to bed. You seemed agitated.

I went to our bedroom and listened to the dull silence break every few minutes whenever you laughed at something he said. I kept thinking: *He's only a guy who works at a bar. He lives off of tips and doesn't have health insurance.* But I knew those things didn't matter sometimes.

I started to say into the pillow, "Come to bed. Come to bed. Come to bed . . ." But you kept laughing. I raised my voice a little. "Come to bed!" I aimed my voice at the two of you. "Come to bed!"

. . .

Your sense of smell is heightened when you drink whiskey. "I love the way you smell," you said, and you pulled me to you, huffing on my shirt and knocking things off the dining room table.

"Really?" I said, thinking I probably stank after a long workday.

"Yes," you said. "You smell so good, so manly."

"I wonder if you're smelling BO." I sniffed my own armpits. "It smells kind of gross to me."

"Oh, you don't even know," you said, shaking your head.

I went into the kitchen and poured you another drink. When I came back to the table your eyes were closed and you were breathing in deep, like you were meditating or something.

"I can smell your penis," you said.

...

"When you were a boy, what did you use for masturbation?" you asked me.

"Besides my hand?" I asked.

"Yes, besides your hand and your Farrah Fawcett poster or whatever."

"It was Loni Anderson," I corrected you. "My mom wouldn't let me have the Farrah poster because her nips were sticking out."

You made an approving sound and took a sip of your tea. We were having our afternoon caffeine at the coffee shop by your library.

I thought about your question for a moment longer and calculated what to say and what to leave out. "I tried to use one of those cardboard toilet paper tubes once," I said.

You grimaced and said, "Well, I guess that's economical, anyway."

"What about you?" I said. "You have to give me one too."

"I used a screwdriver a couple of times," you said. "I thought that's why they called it a screwdriver."

"A couple of times?" I said.

"It wasn't a big pointy one or anything, plus I thought I was doing it wrong or something. I was really worried that my vagina was too big. It was like I was rattling that thing around like someone playing a triangle in a high school band."

"I'm sorry about that," I said. "But I can assure you that your, um, vagina is not too big in any sense."

"Don't try to change the subject," you said.

I looked out the window, off into the shifting light of the

cloudy sky. I searched the depths of my self-abusive lowlights. "We had a really fluffy oven mitt," I finally said. "It was like my secret best friend."

...

I'm not sure if this is okay or not, but I have become almost too casual, perhaps too unselfconscious, around you. I sit on the couch next to you and slip into an array of bad postures. I used to lean back so my stomach looked flatter, but now I pitch forward without thinking. My stomach looks like a giant ball of pizza dough. Sometimes I slap my hand over my belly button to make a pleasing *plop* sound, like a loose bongo. I reach my hand into my pants and maneuver my penis and balls into a more comfortable resting position.

I dramatically pluck hairs out of my nose and aggressively Q-tip my ears. I trim my ugly toenails and I wonder: *Does the grossness of my grooming outweigh the neatness of the end result? Why do I do all of this in front of you?*

If I have to burp, I will not suppress it anymore. If I have to fart, I don't think twice about it. Are these signs that the romance is dead?

I say "excuse me" and "sorry" but you just yawn or laugh at these things. It's like you love me no matter what.

...

I told Vince that he should learn an instrument. "Like a guitar or something," I said. He looked at me suspiciously and his posture deflated. He wanted to know why. "Because it's fun," I said. "Because it helps your math memory," I said. "Because girls like it," I whispered.

"Do you know how to play one?" he asked.

"Yes," I fibbed a little. "Every Good Boy Does Fine."

"What?"

"Every Good Boy Deserves Fudge."

"Is that a band or something?" he said.

"Yes," I lied. "It was a band I used to be in." I was digging some kind of hole for myself to lie in later.

"Were you on the radio? Or *Saturday Night Live*?"

I told him no, we weren't. But I started to imagine what that would have been like. Some quick visions of young groupies danced through my mind.

"What if I played a flute?" he asked.

I tried not to grimace. "Girls don't like flute players," I said.

...

One morning at breakfast, I held your hands on the table as the waitress refilled our coffee. I still felt myself waking up. I liked staring at your hands sometimes. There was something calming about it, like watching a cat sleep on a rug. Your fingers slid between my fingers, your fingernails shorter than mine and chewed down, like little kid fingernails. There was something precise about the weight of your hand in mine. "Squeezy pleasy," I said, and you squeezed my hand, cracking my knuckles. The color of your hands like cream.

...

"I used to fuck girls," your brother, Daniel, told me one night, while we were waiting for you to come home from work. He was already on his fourth beer. I knew he was getting buzzed because he was closing his left eye a lot, like it helped him to think.

"I was pretty good at it," he continued. "But I knew I was just practicing for boys. The first girlfriend I had, when I was a freshman in high school, was a virgin, and for some reason I told her that my dick was nine inches. She didn't really know the difference. She just took my word for it, especially because she was scared to look at it."

I was concerned that the kids might be able to hear him, so I turned up the CD player in the living room. He just raised his own volume more.

"I knew she would talk," he said. "It was genius. I even heard that a few people called me 'Nine,' in like a reverent way, you know? I felt like I got respect, even from some of the popular dudes who never liked me. Of course, those were the ones I wanted the word to get to."

"Daniel," I said, hoping my lowered voice would signal him to be more quiet. He paused for a moment, waiting for me to say more, but I didn't. He was probably waiting for me to ask him how long it really was. But I didn't take the bait.

"Well, I got busted, of course," he finally said. "First, by this senior girl who was kind of a slut, and then by one of the football players." He laughed at this, and I automatically laughed too. "I'll always remember what this girl said. Her name was Cheri, like with a French accent, but she was Mexican. She said to me, 'My last boyfriend had a nine-inch dick and *you* sure don't have nine inches.'"

I thought I heard one of the kids get up, and I looked nervously toward the hallway. Daniel made a little snorting sound and said, "They're not getting up. Don't worry."

"Just be more quiet," I told him. I grabbed a new beer for myself. "What did the football player say?" I asked him.

"Oh, you should have seen it," Daniel said. "He was giving me a hand job and then he suddenly pulled this tape measure out and said, 'I want to see if the rumors are true.' He didn't seem to mind that I fell about three inches short of the mark, but I noticed that people stopped paying attention to me for a while after that. Like my mystique vanished!"

I heard your keys jingle from outside and the front door creaking open. "Little sister's home," Daniel said, and then he whispered, "Act normal."

"What are you bros doing?" you asked.

"Talking about our dicks," Daniel said. "What else would we be doing?"

...

Your friend Karla was getting married to a man fifteen years younger than she was. Also, he was Samoan. I didn't know if there was anything relevant about that fact or not.

"If I was twenty-six, I probably wouldn't mind being with Karla either," I said. I had always liked Karla's look, her long Scandinavian legs and bedroom eyes. "But what happens in ten years? She'll be over fifty and he'll still be young enough to surf and look at women in bikinis all day."

"She'll enjoy it while she can, I guess," you said. "And then maybe she'll move on to someone else."

"You make it sound like she'll be trading in a car," I said.

"I don't think she really cares if it lasts forever or not," you said. "Her friends already know she's crazy, and her parents are dead."

"What does that have to do with anything?" I asked.

"It means she doesn't have to answer to anyone."

I started to envy that about Karla, her fleeting impulses. I wondered if I might be able to have meaningless sex with her someday, just for fun. I almost said something to you about that thought, but I didn't want you to turn the tables on me and say something about having sex with the Samoan. To rephrase the cliché, I wanted to have my cake and smoosh it in your face. And then eat it without giving you any.

You looked like you were daydreaming now too. Maybe about the Samoan, maybe about cake, or maybe about forever.

. . .

We took in a stray cat that we found one day in the grocery store parking lot. At first, we worried that the cat would trigger Vince's allergies, but he didn't have a problem with it. We became enamored with the cat, a large tabby with perfect Tigger-like markings, and we wondered what his past was. One of your friends was a pet psychic and we decided to make her dinner one night so she could tell us more about the cat.

"His name was Peanut, but he didn't like that name very much," the psychic said as she held the cat against her shoulder. "His owner used to live next door, but something bad happened—like a divorce, or maybe someone got arrested—and he was left behind. He doesn't really like to talk about it."

We raised our eyebrows at the word *talk*. But maybe the cat really was talking to her somehow.

"He likes his new name much better. Maybe not Walter but he likes it when you call him Walt. He also feels like you're his family now. He feels a lot of warmth for both of you," said the psychic, and then she looked at me seriously and said, "But your voice bothers him sometimes. He doesn't want you to talk so much."

I stared at the cat and he gave me an uneasy look, as if I had just learned a valuable secret. I started talking loudly, "What is it he doesn't like about my voice? Should I use a singing voice instead? What if I'm just reciting the alphabet, like a, b, c, d, e, f, g, h, i, j, k, l, m, n, o, p . . ."

I watched the cat squirm and claw at the psychic's shoulder.

. . .

I liked going out with my friend Todd because he's six foot three and handsome, and I sensed more women glancing my direction when I was with him. He has blondish-brown hair and is built like a professional tennis player. He's probably my best-looking friend—the kind of guy that all women like, or the kind of guy I would like if I were a woman. When I mentioned Todd to you, though, you shrugged and said that he didn't do anything for you. I almost got defensive. I'm not sure why. I should have felt good that you didn't find him attractive, but I found myself almost pimping him to you. In my own mind, I feel like Todd probably rates close to a ten and I'm a seven on my good days.

"What do you want me to say?" you asked me.

"I want you to tell me the truth," I said. "You don't have to pretend for my benefit."

"You're so shallow," you said. You grabbed my face and looked in my eyes, searching for a sign of anything behind them.

· · ·

There was a time we never really talk about, about six months after we moved in together, when we were going to have separate apartments for the summer. You wanted to live somewhere with a pool, and Maxine was going to be away with her dad. You said you just wanted a little space. We didn't call it a separation or give it any kind of name. Maybe it was a test.

So you moved some of your stuff to a place on the other side of the bridge and went out and bought a new bathing suit.

That summer, you spent one night in your own apartment and the rest with me. You wore your swimsuit only once. You were in the pool for fifteen minutes.

Three months later, you were back at our place. We didn't say anything about the other apartment. You hardly had to clean it when you moved out. It was kind of a joke.

· · ·

There were times when I thought you might be a lesbian and that you'd be happier with a woman. I suggested that you get a female lover and try it out.

I imagined you with a woman, lying poolside after rubbing sunblock on each other, your backs to the sun and your eyes on each other. Or I imagined you and your female partner at Whole Foods, arguing over what kind of bath oil to get. For some reason, I saw her as being tall and a redhead and obsessed with jogging.

You told me no, that's not what you want.

I kept thinking of those ads in the back of the weekly papers: *Are You Bi-Curious?* But you didn't seem curious at all. I realized I was more curious about your sexuality than you were.

...

I have an empty perfume bottle that I took from my first girlfriend a long time ago. We were together for three years. I have very sweet memories of her. She was the first woman I spent the night with, went on trips with, and bought real gifts for. Even though it's empty, I can still smell the way she smelled. Her neck and arms and chest.

I've thought of buying a new bottle of it, either for myself to hide away somewhere or for you to wear, but maybe that's too strange. It's like if you made me wear an old boyfriend's jacket or made your ex-husband's favorite drink for me. We want to brand our own identity, make our own automatic sensory responses.

But I did it anyway. I bought you my first girlfriend's

perfume and pretended I hadn't inhaled it off of someone else's belly before.

You put some on and came close to me. You danced against me in a slow, seductive sway. It really was like an old romantic memory brought back to life. I should have said something or stopped you, but it felt too good. I didn't care if it was wrong. When I closed my eyes, my nose smelled a ghost becoming more real, even if my mind could only picture an empty dress.

...

Did we really worry about other people breaking us up? I thought about this and I knew it would always be possible. Even when I thought about my best characteristic, I knew that someone out there would always be better. I might have good hair, but there is someone who has better hair. There are men with smoother singing voices, whiter teeth, more aptitude with tools and fixing things, and a deeper knowledge of those movies from the fifties that you love.

Did you worry about all the women with bigger tits, more tanned skin, an enthusiasm for basketball, and a sweeter morning disposition?

There are men with bigger cocks out there. I've seen them on my computer screen.

Maybe I'm not funny enough. You'd find someone funnier than I am.

You knew I had developed a thing for Asian girls. Did that worry you? Were you afraid you weren't Asian enough? Do you even have any Asians in your family?

When I thought about these things, I just wanted to close my eyes and hold you for several minutes, preferably lying down. Then I wanted to feel my spirit float to the ceiling as I started over with my thoughts.

I wanted to become a room full of air for you to breathe in.

Then we got the tweezers and fixed each other's eyebrows. Then you'd plucked the hairs out of my nose.

. . .

Sometimes when we were out somewhere, you'd catch me looking at other women. I'd watch them walk by and my head would follow them for a few seconds, like a camera. Then I'd look back at you and you'd shake your head with a disapproving grimace. "What?" I'd say.

"I can always tell when you're checking someone out because your leg starts to shake and you do this funny thing with your tongue," you told me.

"You make me sound like some kind of dog," I said.

Sometimes when men walked by, I watched them as well, for the same reason. Sometimes I liked the way they dressed or I wondered what they looked like naked. You didn't say anything when I looked at men. They weren't perceived as a threat to us.

I watched couples too. There were beautiful ones and there were mismatched ones. Ugly guys and cute girls. Dumpy-looking women and handsome men. I tried to figure out the tricky math between everyone, how we all equaled the same things.

...

There was a box of beignet mix from Café du Monde in my cupboard that had been there for over a year. We bought it while we were in New Orleans the year before but we never got around to making them. The box was gold and brown and had a classic illustration of the famous café on it. The instructions were in French and English and said that the beignets were best with their "delicious Creole coffee with chicory." It was far beyond the expiration date. I took it out and put it on a shelf above the sink because I didn't want to throw it out. I pretended it was like a decoration.

...

Vince was talking to his new friend Roberto on the cordless phone in his room. You and I were outside his door, trying to figure out what they were talking about. We caught little bits of Vince's side of the conversation. "You should have paintball at your next birthday party . . . Yeah, I don't really like birthday parties anymore either . . . I shot a BB gun before . . . Have you ever had Hawaiian pizza before? . . . I always pick the Canadian bacon off . . . I can't stand that crap . . .

We looked at each other, a little shocked at his harsh criticism of Canadian bacon. Then his voice got quieter and I thought I heard him say, "Fuck that guy" or maybe "Fuckin' A" or maybe "Fuckin' Dave," and then he said, "Shit," and laughed. Your eyes got big and you frantically motioned me to the kitchen.

"Did he say the words *fuckin' gay*?" you asked me.

"I don't think so," I said. "But he definitely used the F-word."

Your mouth was still shocked open. We hardly ever swore around the kids, but I knew there was a lot of that at school. Even when we walked by the Catholic school down the street, we would hear fourth graders spouting gangsta rap lyrics. Plus, we had watched a stand-up comedy show on HBO recently.

"Should we talk to him about this?" you asked.

"Maybe," I said reluctantly. "I don't think he talks like that all the time though. It sounds like he's just trying it out."

"Maybe we need to meet this Roberto and make sure he's not a bad influence."

We heard Vince laugh again. It sounded a little fake.

"Do you think Maxine talks like that?" you asked.

"I heard her say *bitch* before," I answered.

You shrugged your shoulders, like that wasn't a big deal.

...

We were house-sitting for a friend of a friend. We didn't know this man personally. We were told that he was an artist of some kind and he was in another city preparing an art show for the next month. He had a garden we were supposed to tend and a bird to feed.

We even stayed there a few nights, because it was in a nicer neighborhood than ours. After about a week, we became curious and started snooping through his stuff.

From the clothes in his closet, we figured out that he was a small man. But there was one drawer in his dresser where we found several pairs of extra large boxer shorts and T-shirts.

In his medicine cabinet, we found the usual pills and Band-Aids but also bottles of medicine with strange names and long, complicated instructions. You sampled some of them.

We found the key to the basement and walked down the creaky steps. We discovered a makeshift stage with cameras and lights surrounding it. Over to the side was a tall black filing cabinet that we rifled through. In it, we found a series of photos that featured a statuesque lady in her fifties. She looked glamorous but very serious and powerfully broad-shouldered. For some reason, my first thought was that may-be she was a famous opera singer. As we looked through these photos, we found several where she was standing next to the man we were house-sitting for. We could see, even though she was nearly twice his size and probably ten years older, that they were lovers. They held hands, leaned against each other, and even smiled, mid laugh, as the shutter froze them for eternity.

The more we looked, though, the less they smiled. She began to look older and weaker but the man looked the same in every picture. Then there were photos of the woman hold-ing the man's cat, photos of her with other people we didn't recognize, photos of her wearing masks and wigs, and pho-tos of her naked and crouched. We finally realized that these cameras, this room, captured a woman gradually dying.

We put everything back the way we found it. We went upstairs and locked the door. Everything had the smell and feeling of death from then on. You considered every object a bit longer, as if it could somehow infect you. I didn't even want to sleep in the bedroom.

For some reason, we forgot about the love we saw in the photos. The only thing that stuck with us was how easily life faded away in front of us.

...

In the middle of the night, you were slowly running your fingers down my stomach and woke me up. You couldn't fall asleep and asked me for help. "Take an Ambien," I said. Most of the time, I didn't like it when you took pills, but I was too tired to argue about it sometimes.

"I can't," you said. "I'm on a diet, and it'll make me eat."

"You don't need to diet. Don't be crazy," I said.

You kept touching me. I was getting hard, but I was too tired. Plus, I had masturbated earlier that night.

"But look at my stomach. I look pregnant," you said. You stuck your belly out as far as it would go.

"I'm more pregnant than you," I said, cupping my belly with both hands and rubbing it like a crystal ball.

Then you started talking about something that was going to take a long time to talk about. I can't even remember what it was, but I was trying to avoid it like a dodgeball.

I turned away from you, hoping that you would get the hint. "I gotta sleep," I said. "One of us has to be awake for the kids in the morning."

You got quietly sullen for a while. I could always tell your sullen quiet from your normal quiet—your sullen quiet had a buzz to it, like a television showing a tornado tearing houses apart, but with the volume turned down. Then I heard your voice start whispering. It was like that for a while, soft and un-threatening, like you were just talking to yourself. But then you swerved into a field of questions. I didn't understand what they were—I was half asleep already—but I could hear how you whispered them, like a subliminal spy digging for subconscious thoughts. You tried to make the inflection of the question marks sound sweet, undetectable. Your hands stayed away from me. I simply slurred, over and over, "It's okay. It'll be okay." I figured that could be the answer to any of your questions.

...

Vince told me he was meeting a friend to see a movie. I asked if it was Roberto and he said yes, but also two other friends named Serena and Elise. I wondered if this was a double date.

He needed a ride, so I told him I'd take him. I really hoped to meet the other kids, but it was at a theater in the mall, so I just dropped him off outside with a twenty-dollar bill and told him I'd meet him at the arcade next to the theater at 7:00 PM.

I fought off the urge to come back to the movie and sit in the back row to spy on them. I wasn't sure if I could sit through the movie version of *The A-Team* anyhow.

When I got to the arcade later, I met Serena. She was nervous and had dark goth hair and sad eyes. She wore clip-on earrings and a fake leather jacket that looked like it would be too warm for the weather. I gave Vince a five-dollar bill to change into quarters, and they played a fighting game with various buttons and two joysticks. Their hands flew everywhere, sweaty and suddenly competitive. I played the lonely Pac-Man and pinball machines.

Serena's dad showed up about twenty minutes later, and I spoke to him for a moment, but he also seemed nervous. He was at least ten years older than me and looked Italian, unlike Serena. It almost seemed like he didn't speak English, or maybe the noise was too loud around us.

When we all walked out to the parking garage, the fresh air cleared my head. Serena's dad was still silent, so I asked Vince if Roberto and Elise were also at the movie. "No," Vince said quickly.

"Who?" asked Serena.

"Nothing," said Vince.

"What about Elise?" Serena asked.

"I'll tell you later," said Vince. I saw his face go white, like he was caught in a lie, or something else sticky and sensitive.

"How was the movie?" I finally thought to ask.

"It was awesome," said Vince. "It was all right," said Serena at the same time. It sounded like: *It was awesright.*

I wondered if they would go on another date, but I didn't want to pester Vince about it. I stood in his doorway a few days later and told Vince he could talk to me about girls if he ever wanted to. I felt like an actor in a TV show when I said that.

. . .

Vince was eating his pancakes plain. I offered him some maple syrup but he shook his head.

"What's wrong?" I said. "Are you depressed about something?"

"No," he said.

"Only depressed people eat their pancakes plain," I told him.

He picked up the syrup and poured a tiny bit on.

"Well, I'm glad you're not *totally* depressed," I said.

. . .

I took the day off work and made the kids' lunches and sent them off to school. After they left, we talked about what there was to do. There were piles of DVDs from the library, but we were bored of all those recommendations from your coworkers. We didn't have any money to spend, and our bank accounts were dangerously close to zero. Our cable had been turned off, so we took turns giving each other massages and looking for the strangest porn we could find on the Internet (we had worried about our Internet being turned off just the previous day but couldn't stand the thought of that, so we borrowed sixty dollars from your dad to pay the bill). We had sex twice. And then a third time that didn't seem to satisfy you.

You said that I was tuned out and that I wasn't looking at you like a person. I told you I wasn't objectifying you, but in a way I was. I had started in that third time to see if I could still do it. I remembered a time when we could have sex three or four times in one day. That was before we lived together.

You asked me why I'd wanted to do it a third time anyway. I told you that I got excited when you put your hair up and started making lunch. You were naked, but you put a red apron on while you stirred some meatballs into a pan of sauce. There was a large pot with spaghetti boiling, and the steam surrounded you like a magic trick. The truth was that you simply looked different. In fact, you looked kind of like the new girl at work. The one I haven't worked up the nerve to talk to. The one with the expensive-looking wedding ring. The lesbian girl at work said that she also had pierced nipples. She had seen her at her health club, in the showers.

I started imagining that I was the lesbian and you were the nipple-pierced woman. I had you pressed against the wall, steam floating by. I was a butch, with a rubber cock that never gave up and never got soft. I stared at your nipples and pierced them in my mind. You said, "Hey. Don't fuck me like I'm just some *body*."

The meat and sauce burned in the pan. You started scraping it all out when we were done. I told you that it was just the bottom that was burned. Everything else was fine. Everything else was actually great. I ate a whole plateful, trying to prove myself to you.

...

Sometimes I would start to say something and you'd cut me off, or we'd be with a bunch of friends and they would all be talking over me. I'm very soft-spoken, so this happens a lot. I say a couple of words, and then my voice is buried. I wonder if anyone ever hears me. Sometimes, even when we were somewhere quiet, I would say half of a sentence and stop, just to see if you were paying attention. "What were you saying?" I hoped you'd ask.

But maybe you thought muttering half sentences was how I spoke—my own personal pattern of speech. Or maybe you didn't need many clues to what I was thinking.

Sometimes, when these thoughts were running through my brain, you'd be saying something to me but I wouldn't be listening.

. . .

If we were arguing about something and I was wrong, I would eventually admit it. And if you were wrong, you would usually surrender too. But if we were both wrong, it would go on forever, because neither of us wanted to be the first to give in. I couldn't think of any sentences for my mouth, just small, failing statements that squatted between parentheses in my brain. They'd never stand up straight and move forward. We gave each other the silent treatment until something indefinable cracked between us. Something larger than language.

. . .

We started bickering over small household things, too. I always thought you had the heat up too much and if I turned it down, you'd get mad and pretend like you were freezing. I slept in only boxers, you slept in layers—long-sleeve T-shirt, shorts, pajama top and bottoms, sometimes even a sweater and scarf. I told you that I feared you'd strangle yourself at night.

We fought over the lights too. I liked the apartment bright so I could see what I was eating for dinner, see whatever I was trying to read on the couch. You'd come into the living room and grimace, like the brightness was killing you. You'd turn off the overhead light and turn on a dim lamp instead.

If I had an open bag of chips somewhere, you'd eat them all or throw them out and then yell at me for not hiding them better.

I could not fold bedsheets correctly, according to you.

I complained about your organic peanut butter.

The kids started in on each other too—Maxine getting upset at Vince for being in the bathroom too long. Vince saying she hogged the TV.

These small battles seemed silly and innocuous at first, but they eventually bugged me more and more, like small buzzing flies in front of my face.

...

At a certain point in our third year, you were getting bored and didn't know what to do with yourself. Your hours at the library were cut and you were working only three days a week. You became depressed and stopped doing the things that you enjoyed doing. I tried to help by giving you things to do on your days off, lists to cross out, recreational "lunchtime" video clips to watch. You slogged through the day without giving a thought to any of it. When I came home at night, work-beaten and starved, I asked you if you'd done any of the things I'd asked you to do. You said no and blew out a sigh that sounded like an inflatable boat sinking in a muddy river.

I couldn't even make you laugh. There was a Ziploc bag of Chinese herbs in my coat pocket that I kept forgetting to take out. It had been in there for a week and had somehow gotten wet and become gooey. Whenever I fished my fingers in there to look for something, they came out looking like I had dipped them in shit. But they smelled good, so I didn't wash my hands right away. I walked around the apartment waiting for you to notice.

When it was time for bed, we brushed our teeth, side by side, looking in the mirror. We used to exchange sweet glances until things started to feel different. Then you stared straight ahead, watching your mouth turn foamy. I stared so hard at myself I couldn't see anything.

...

It was unseasonably warm outside, and we were having sex as the sun slowly went down. It was the first time we'd done it in almost two weeks. An old country song was on the radio.

"Do you love me?" I asked.

You didn't say anything. The humidity made it hard even to breathe.

"Say you love me," I said a minute later.

You wouldn't look me in the eyes. Our love making didn't feel like an emotional reconnection so much as it felt like a response to some kind of mental pressure to end our sex drought. It didn't truly feel like making love. It was more like we were falling back into our roles. Reluctant romance.

Maybe we were just tired. What we wanted and what we could give were two different things that seemed so far away from each other.

"Can't you say the words?" I asked you.

I felt you tense up.

"Do you not love me?" I whispered.

"I don't," you said. A swallow of air like a hiccup. "I don't want to."

There were shadows on the wall eating each other. Even the flies were suffocating around us.

When we were done, I noticed the old country song, still on the radio. Then it finally ended.

· · ·

One of your friends said we should go see her therapist for couples counseling. I always thought we kept up a happy facade, that we were normal in most senses. But your friend said that even happy couples are fucked up.

We made an appointment and I started to compile a list of things we could talk about. You did the same.

At the first therapy session, we went down our lists. The unearthing of these concerns, these nuisances or trivial peeves, gave new weight to things I thought we really didn't care about, like cleaning the apartment or buying needless things at the grocery store. But we were merely throwing pebbles at each other.

Then your pebbles turned into giant boulders—heavy, abstract things I didn't know how to catch or deflect. You said, "Sometimes I feel like you're listening to me, but you're not hearing what I'm saying."

I had to space out each word in my brain to piece together the puzzle of your statement. While I was doing that, I didn't hear the next four minutes of your list.

The therapist sat with her folded hands in her lap. Her long face and feathered gray hair made me think of a horse, staring at us in a meadow.

You had moved on to the time I got mad at you for breaking my computer.

I tried to jump in with something to slow you down. "What about the time you yelled at me about how to stretch out my leather shoes? I told you that my friend Michelle said to spray them with water and you freaked out and called Michelle a stupid lesbian. Do you remember how unnecessarily angry that whole conversation was?"

"But that was when I was crazy," you said. "That was when I was between meds. You can't use that against me. And it's still not the right way to deal with leather shoes!"

"And what about the time you wouldn't ride in my dad's Fiat?"

"That was also when I was between meds. And that thing was a death trap."

Everything I said after that was tossed aside with the same answer: "Between meds."

I realized that maybe you were right and your temperament was normal now. All of my pebbles (and a few rocks) were coming at you from days long gone. You were able to rewrite history, like Zoloft could make the rough patches of the past well-intentioned and smooth.

The therapist looked at me with an accusing glare as I stammered. I was simply the one without an excuse.

We shook the therapist's hand as we left. I knew we'd be coming back for more.

...

I kept a journal during our therapy period. Most of the entries are written with a steady hand, easy to read, and often in very direct language, as if I knew how to steer my head and my heart at the same time. But I was faking it.

In reality, my head and my heart were big, lumbering automobiles, careening toward the same parking spot right before they ran out of gas. They were completely separate entities— smoking violently and moaning like old machinery.

The only places in my journal where you might be able to detect this conflict are the parts where the handwriting becomes sloppy. The words are scrawled, as if in a code. Like that serial killer who taunted the newspaper editors and practically begged them to catch him. But my bad handwriting is too scared to taunt. It does not know which side to choose. It can't be read. In this way, it served to protect me.

...

After what turned out to be our last appointment with that therapist, we were driving home, and I told you that I wanted to move out for a while. Your face turned dark and angry and I thought you might hit me. "Don't," I said.

You took off your seat belt and curled into a ball in the passenger seat. Your body slumped down and you trembled with your face in your hands. I felt like breaking down too, but your reaction made me turn stoic for some reason. "It'll be better for both of us," I said.

"Why?" you said.

"I don't know," I said. "It's just how I feel right now."

"I don't want to stay there," you said. "We'll move out. You and Vince can stay there."

Besides the emotional drain of a breakup, I realized at this moment that there was a physical drag to it as well—the moving-out part. For some reason, I almost felt worse about Maxine having to move out.

I kept driving down the freeway. I noticed the radio was still on and there was a diamond commercial on. I turned it down, but not off. I started to talk. "Maybe this is just a good time to see if . . ." I trailed off and didn't know what I wanted to say.

"Don't speak to me unless you have something fucking clear to say," you said through your tears.

"I'm sorry," I said. "I love you."

"You're just talking at it, not working at it," you said.

My head felt light, almost weightless. Someone honked at me for driving too slow. I felt like stopping right there. A man swerved around me, his head out of his window, yelling, "What the hell are you doing, asshole?"

. . .

Two days later, before you moved out, you told me that you simply wanted someone to "love the hell out of you." I said I did—I loved the hell out of you and the shit out of you and the holy fuck out of you. But still, you wanted more than words that were simply repeated and riffed on. I felt like I had to get on my hands and knees for you. I had to come up with other words that would crawl to you, like soldiers on a battlefield.

But you wanted actions, you said. You made the word sound long in the air between us—"Aaaaaccc-ssshhhuuunnsss"—so maybe I would grab it.

...

All the things we'd talked about doing—*poof!*—suddenly gone. My mind felt blank and my heartbeat seemed to fluctuate every hour.

This confused me. One moment I would feel like collapsing to my knees and a few minutes later, I'd want to jump up and down. I would remind myself that I was free. For some reason, these feelings of untethered freedom would most often emerge while I was driving somewhere. I whooped and hollered with the windows rolled up, like a crazy person.

Then I'd feel myself deflate again.

...

You and Maxine decided to leave for California. You said it would be for two months, or you might stay down there. I was sad to see Maxine, in the passenger seat, staring straight ahead and not even speaking to me before you drove off. I wondered if our breakup would damage her somehow. Maybe she would believe in love a little bit less because of what happened with us.

A few days later, I put your things in storage, not sure if I'd see you again. That was one of the hardest days of my life, loading up that storage space and sending you the key in the mail.

Two weeks after that, I was already restless and didn't know what to do with myself. I began seeing a woman who worked at the grocery store down the street. She had made a comment about a bottle of wine I was buying one night, "Save some for me," she said. I started to daydream about her before I even left the store.

Her name was Lucy, and we went out every other night after that. There were two new bars that she liked to go to. A place called the Tiger Bar and another place named Spirits. We did this for almost a month, ending some nights with slow, sad make-out sessions in my car. Then I found out that she was married to a soldier in Iraq. She acted like I was the person in the wrong and gave me a long lecture before breaking off our relationship.

...

I started dating a woman sixteen years younger than I was. She was barely drinking age. When you found out about this through a friend, you asked me if I was a pedophile. I knew you said this out of spite, so I tried not to acknowledge it. But the question did linger with me for an uncomfortable moment.

I showed this girl a lot of things I liked. Music, movies, food. After a while, it felt like I was teaching her, guiding her, molding her into the shape of something I wanted.

Maybe she could just be a younger version of you. But I began to resent all of the work I was doing.

"Show me something *you* like," I said to her once. And she showed me something I liked. "Show me something *only you* like," I said.

"I don't know what I like," she said, getting flustered.

I had to break up with her.

That was when I felt like I wanted to start seeing you again. Like I needed to see you. You had moved back to Portland and told me in an email about a great deal you got on an apartment.

You let me come over to this apartment, soon after. It was on the other side of town and felt like a long drive. When I first walked in I noticed that it smelled like leather boots. You always had new leather boots. You had new things to show me. Things I'd never seen before. I didn't have to teach you a thing. You were already taught and prepared.

...

You used to waive any library late fees I had, but you stopped doing that after we broke up. It was a small thing, but it felt like a grudge. A slap on my wrist that left a brief red mark and a sting. I'd return my late books and CDs to another library so you wouldn't see me.

...

You called me early in the morning and said, "Let me think out loud for a second." I rubbed my eyes and looked at the clock. I couldn't tell if it said six or eight. I thought maybe I was dreaming.

"If we had a baby together, I think our lives would be very confusing," you said.

I started to say something, but you shushed me. "Be quiet," you said. "I'm thinking." And then you told me about the last-second shot in the basketball game you went to the night before. And then you wondered who was on the *Today* show and then started talking about breakfast. You really were thinking out loud. I sat up in bed and laid my cell phone on my blanketed belly. I put it on speakerphone and listened to your unedited thoughts spilling out on my lap. It was like I'd cut off your head but it still kept talking.

. . .

I liked the idea of a third child. It would be a combination of the two of us. But I wondered if the very idea of our own child would damage the other kids. It might create a sense of half-ness that they wouldn't have known before. They might feel like the separate halves. The lost halves.

. . .

You had a dream that I was a bright-green spider about the size of a tennis ball. You usually hate spiders, but you said I looked too exotic to kill, so you slid me onto a morning newspaper and took me to the back porch. You set me down in a sunny spot, and I crawled away from you slowly, sometimes stopping and looking behind me.

You almost wanted to crush me, but you said there would be too much blood. Too much of a *crunch* sound and gross green fluid.

You said I went to the edge of the lawn and parted the blades of grass like curtains. Your eyes hovered after me, following me like helicopters. You said you woke up missing me.

...

There was a woman named Joan I dated twice. She bored me by constantly trying to be funny. I laughed only to humor her, and because she was desirable. We came close to having sex but didn't. A couple of months later, she emailed me and told me I was boring. She said I had the strained expression of someone who wanted to kill himself but couldn't gather the courage. She said I was a threat to her happiness.

...

I saw your brother, Daniel, walking on Hawthorne Boulevard and I crossed the street to avoid him. I wasn't sure how he felt about our situation and I didn't want a confrontation.

Maybe this moment of fear grew out of something that happened to me when I was twenty and a girl I had just broken up with sent her brother to my place to beat me up. The girl's brother was smaller than I was but he still managed to punch me several times before I could fight him off.

I went into a vintage clothing store and looked at shoes for ten minutes until I thought it was probably safe to leave, but as I was getting ready to leave, I saw Daniel walking in. I hid behind a rack of belts. I watched Daniel looking at suit jackets and then I saw him take out his phone and text someone. He was frowning as he did so. I wondered if he was texting you. I wondered if maybe you would walk in soon. This was during a bad week for us, when we were trying to avoid each other.

I waited for Daniel to turn around so I could sneak out. He picked up a jacket and walked to a mirror to try it on. I walked toward the door and glanced over to see him. It looked like he was posing in the mirror, hands on his hips, one knee bent, chin up. He saw me in the mirror but didn't turn around. I stopped for some reason and waved half-heartedly at him, like I'd been caught. He relaxed his pose and smiled. He winked.

I left without saying a word.

. . .

I wanted to call you when I was crying, so you could hear it. I knew it would be selfish, but I wanted you to have some of the pain.

Some days, when we were with each other and we were crying together, it almost felt good. Like we were making love again.

If the day comes when you can't make me cry, it means I've been worn out too much—too many highs and lows might eventually turn me numb. No more tears will mean I don't love you anymore.

. . .

I wanted to see how long I could go without texting or calling you. It was like seeing how long I could hold my breath underwater. It made my neck tense and my shoulders scrunch. My body coil up.

When I had to interact with people at the hotel, I didn't smile so much. I bit the inside of my cheek and hoped my face formed a pleasant shape.

…

You said you only smoke cigarettes after sex. I saw you in your car with a guy I thought was your cousin, stopped at a red light, exhaling smoke.

…

Sometimes, when you were upset, I'd be afraid to ask what I could do. You sometimes snapped at me and said, "If you really loved me, you'd know what to do."

I've always thought this was an unfair belief. Some kind of theory that has never been scientifically proven. Because I do really love you, and I still never know what to do.

…

We saw each other at a housewarming party when we were separated. Our friends became tense, like we were going to get in a fight right there in front of the chips and salsa and baby carrots. But we just smiled at each other and stayed civil.

It was a grown-up party, with soft music, button-up shirts, and children sleeping upstairs.

Your friends swarmed around you, like they wanted to hustle you out of there. You held your hands up to them, as if to say, *Calm down. I'm okay.*

My friends, many of them mutual friends of ours, didn't swarm me, but they did move closer. They looked at me, subtle and sideways. Then they looked at you, grimacing. Then they looked at me again. They were trying to translate what was happening in the air between us.

We were there for most of the night but didn't speak to each other. It was like that game we played sometimes, where we put our faces as close together as possible without actually kissing (we called it "movie kiss"). You looked good—a little different, somehow. I wondered if you felt different too. I looked the same as I always do. People started to leave, but we stayed. My hands began to sweat, but my head felt good, a slight buzz giving me a new social confidence.

Around midnight, one of the hosts, a new mom named Maureen, went upstairs and returned minutes later with her six-month-old boy. "Look who woke up for the party," she said. The baby looked wide awake. His sea-blue eyes were the brightest thing in the room, and his mouth bent into a smirking half-smile. He lapped up some fawning affection from the remaining party guests and then turned his attention to his mother's blouse. He grabbed at her buttons and bra.

The last few friends said their rushed good nights, leaving you and me as the final stragglers. The husband of the house said he wanted to give us some of the leftover desserts.

"To bring home to your kids," he said. We stood there, still without a word between us, waiting for him to Tupperware the cake and pie. We saw Maureen sit down and lower her bra strap, then we turned away shyly.

"Look how hungry he is," Maureen said. She was inviting us to look, so we turned and watched. I stared at the baby's small mouth, the cheeks sucking in and out. I noticed his eyes slowly closing in peace and Maureen's eyes following suit. "He's been partial to the left one," she said with a quick laugh. "I think it's sweeter on that side."

We watched the baby feed for a few more minutes, and then the husband came out of the kitchen with our take-home treats in one container. He stood next to us, happy and tired. I let my right hand open up and float closer to yours. You reached out and grabbed it. We held hands until we got outside. We still didn't say a word, but we smiled before we let go and got into our cars.

...

I saw you out with someone else, and for some reason it didn't bother me as much as I thought it might. He was taller than me, but slouched and thinner. His glasses were sleek and expensive-looking. I came to some unexpected realization that it would be okay if we weren't together for a while, even if that "while" became permanent. I somehow thought—and maybe even felt—that we would do what was best for both of us. What was best for the kids was still a mystery.

But then I went to your new apartment and spent a couple of uncomfortable hours talking to you. We had trouble verbalizing what we wanted in our lives, as if the bridge between us was already burned.

Then, before I left, we hugged, and you held on to me longer than I expected. You made some soft, breathy sounds, and I couldn't help but get hard. It had been almost three months since we touched. You started to kiss me and we walked instinctively—me forward, you backward—our mouths still stuck together, into your bedroom. We took our clothes off quickly, before I remembered the person I had seen you with. I wasn't sure if this was a new guy you were dating or even if you'd had sex with him, but I started to imagine you with him, even as I went down on you. I thought, at that moment, that's what we both wanted—for a third party to rewire our circuits, to lessen the pressure of our overflow. I wanted to see you suck another man's cock, your head turned to the side, his belly against your forehead. I would slide inside you and fuck you hard enough to watch your tits bounce.

It was the first time I had thought about you as something less than a lover. Or maybe more than a lover.

...

"I like how memories work," I said.

"I don't," you said. "It's annoying. Everything reminds me of you."

We were talking on the phone, trying to pretend we weren't hashing things out.

"I listen to Mazzy Star and it reminds me of you," I said.

"I don't like it," you said.

"You don't like Mazzy Star?"

"No. I mean I don't like that it reminds me of you. And that movie. And that book. And that ice cream place. And this shirt. Even my fucking car reminds me of you."

"Your car?" I asked.

"Yes, my car. No matter what I'm doing."

"Go on a road trip with someone else, then," I said.

"I can't transfer memories off to someone else," you said.

There was a long pause.

"You got to do all that stuff first with me," you said. "You got here first."

. . .

There was a night when I wanted to see you but you weren't answering your phone. I drove by the library to see if you were working. I sat in my car, in the parking lot across the street. I was parked next to a big truck, partially obscured so you might not see me when you came out. Your car was parked just down the street. When I drove by it, I was tempted to stop for a moment and peek into it, just to see what was inside. Maybe I'd see a book or CD or something that would signal how you were feeling lately.

The library had just closed and it was getting dark outside and I had my engine off. My radio was on at low volume, playing some sad new folk band's song. I just wanted to see you walk out to your car, see what you were wearing, maybe listen to you talk to a coworker, say good night the way you say good night ("g'night"). I waited for twenty minutes and you hadn't come out. The small parking lot I was in was next to some kind of medical building. There was a dumpster off to my left and I saw a group of rats scurrying around. They were tearing apart a white garbage bag of something. They were making a mess. If I had had a gun or a slingshot I could have shot them. I could have done some damage. But they didn't even know I was there.

I waited another ten minutes and saw two other library employees leave but not you. I turned my car on and eased out of the parking lot with my headlights off. The rats stopped what they were doing and sat staring at me. I rolled my window down about halfway and gave the one with the biggest chunk of bag a nod, as if to say, *It's cool, man. This will be our little secret.*

I took a wide, slow, mulling route through the next neighborhood and then drove by the library again to see that your car was gone. I wondered if you had seen me parked there and made your escape after I left. I pulled back into the parking lot for some reason—maybe to see what the rats were doing. They weren't around anymore either. I made little kissy sounds out the window, like I was trying to call them back. "Where did everyone go?" I heard myself say.

...

When we lived together—when we fell asleep and woke up together in *our* bed—we made love. That's what we called it.

When we found ourselves apart, it turned into something different. An uncertainty and desperation strangled us like a choke chain. We had to settle for just fucking. There was no sleeping and no waking up. No beginning and no ending. We tried to work our way out of the middle of our mess.

...

It felt so strange to be in the apartment with just Vince. And when he was at his mom's, it was just me. There were days when I felt an exciting sense of freedom that I hadn't felt in years. I tried to remember the last time I wasn't in a relationship or living with someone. Maybe when I was twenty-one.

I had a dream one night that I was on an inner tube attached to a big boat by a long rope. Everyone on the boat was having a good time but would sometimes look out to the water and frown in my direction. Eventually, the rope became untied and I drifted off by myself. I looked around and saw no sign of land.

"Hey, Dad," Vince called to me from his room one day. It was a Friday, but there was no school. "What are we going to do today?" he asked me.

I didn't know how to answer. My mind could not lock onto anything. Then I noticed that he still had a photograph of him and Maxine on his dresser. They were sitting on a Ferris wheel, holding hands. My heart squeezed tight in my chest. "I'm sorry, Vince," I said. I started to cry and sat on his bed. I put my hand on his leg. "I'm so sorry," I said softly. "I don't know what I'm doing. I'm screwing things up."

We sat like that for a while and I started to wonder if crying in front of your son was a bonding experience or a traumatic one. I was on the verge of hyperventilating. He was looking down at my hand on his leg. "It's okay," he said. "Things will turn out," he said.

I wasn't sure where he'd heard that expression before. Maybe from me. We plopped back on his bed and lay side by side. "Let's just rest for a moment," I said. "Let's look at your ceiling together."

I noticed a bunch of plastic glow-in-the-dark stars that I had stuck up there when we first moved in. I had forgotten all about them. I wondered if they still glowed, if they still worked.

. . .

I would get dizzy in the morning. I forgot to eat sometimes, and then someone would say, "You look like you're losing weight," and I'd think to myself: *Oh, yeah. Food.*

I'd get shaky. I would see little ghostlike shapes (glow-in-the-dark moths) in the periphery of my vision, like I was tripping on mushrooms. I'd sit on the toilet and notice a pattern on the bathroom rug. It was a Persian rug full of circular flower and ornamental leaf designs. One part of it looked like a face with an O-shaped mouth. I imagined it saying, "Eat a banana. Eat some vegetables."

I made Vince his school lunch. It was uninspired: half of an almond butter and jelly sandwich, a granola bar, and an apple. I knew he probably didn't care, but I imagined his disappointment and it made me depressed.

I ate one bite of leftover scrambled eggs and called it good. I told myself that it was okay to be hungry.

...

When we were apart, the hardest part of the day was waking up. I'd stand in the shower, letting the morning fog in my head clear away as I peed down the drain and wondered if I had a clean towel to use. I would feel tired, sad, and dull.

I tried to think of things I was lucky to have: a loving son and a decent job and I wasn't sure what else. It would be all too easy to let those things slip too. As a single parent, I felt that I lacked the strength and creativity required to raise my young son. I needed help with him, and I feared that he would become bored or distant from me, maybe taking up with the other wild screeching kids around the neighborhood, roaming the alleys and mini-marts like packs of wolves. At work, I was becoming unfocused and letting things slip. I was showing up late and unshaved, and I wasn't saving guest reservations properly in the computer. One day, I lost a couple's luggage for an hour and made them late for the airport.

I had no idea what other job I could even get if I were fired. There was an old Pepsi-Cola bottling company down the street from me and I always thought I'd have to get a job there if everything fell apart. This imaginary me, wearing a Pepsi uniform and driving a forklift or loading a big truck, would be my lowest low. And if I ever did fall to that, a soulless factory kind of job that barely paid me enough to get me by, I also could see myself eventually failing even more and becoming homeless. Then I'd really be down to zero. I would look back at this numb time in the shower and feel like I had been extremely fortunate even to have had what I had—a half-empty apartment and a refrigerator with four or five items in it.

I tried to ignore the cold feeling of the air around me as I turned off the water.

...

There were days when I was so close to tears that I didn't know what to do. I walked around, feeling hollow, off-balance. I went to the mall and floated through it aimlessly, hoping that something could swing my emotional state one way or the other. I went to the bathroom and stared into the mirror to see if that would do anything. It just made my eyes hurt.

I sat outside the lingerie shop and let my mind wonder about the women walking in and out, but my emotional state remained flat. I sensed a bunch of vague mental hurdles that I needed to jump over, but it wasn't happening.

Then I made my way to the toy store and listened to the sounds around me—the excited shouts and the occasional temper tantrum—and it finally came. I made awful creaking wheezes with my throat and my nose ran sloppy with tears and dripping snot.

After I cleaned myself up (the cashiers came quick with the Kleenex), I wandered down to the music store and found a listening station with the most American rock 'n' roll I could find.

...

When I wasn't feeling depressed, I would have random moments of euphoria. I would be driving my car, excited that my future could be open, untethered to someone, and I would loudly sing along to the music on the radio. I would drum the steering wheel and punch the roof, the road ahead of me without stop signs or streetlights or speed traps. I would fantasize about arriving at a house in the middle of nowhere, all its windows open with curtains fluttering in the warm breeze, where a beautiful woman I'd never seen before would have sex with me without any strings attached. Then I'd get in my car and drive away as this woman—someone who couldn't speak English, perhaps—leaned exhausted against her front door, mouthing words that I couldn't and didn't need to understand.

...

Should we have considered this "breakup" a draw? Didn't we both raise our white flags and wave them blindly at each other?

I never thought that you were as unstable as I was. I never knew if we were secure enough to look past all our combined baggage.

Was it sometimes best to ignore certain weaknesses? Did we pretend the scars weren't there? I learned that some things couldn't ever add up. Scars plus Time still equals Scars. Your mom had said to you before she died, "Scars last forever, but so does love."

You wanted to move back in with me. You moved back in.

We tried to focus on the positive. We tried to ignore the negative. We realized that nothing would be perfect. I wondered in my mind what Time plus Imperfection equaled, but I couldn't care, couldn't dwell on it. I was tired of math.

You appeared in my bed again at night. Things felt better that way. Life fell back into some kind of order. It was a start. A new start.

. . .

When you moved back into the apartment, I knew that it wouldn't be good to separate again. Our commitment had to be deeper this time around.

One night you wanted to take me out for a reunion drink. "This new place I found looks really cute," you said, driving my car. We pulled into the parking lot for Spirits.

"Oh," I said.

I couldn't tell you that I'd been there before, with the wife of a soldier. It would have just caused an unnecessary fight. We went inside and I made sure we sat in a corner booth, where I could keep my eye on the door in case Lucy came in.

I liked Spirits a lot, but I had to make a sacrifice. I started complaining about everything. I said my drink was too weak. I made fun of the jukebox, the neon lights, the other customers.

When we left, you said, "Well, I guess we won't be going back there."

We got in the car and I said, "Let's go to Holman's." That was the place we usually went to, so you said okay.

"What's this place called again?" I asked, pulling out of the parking lot.

"Spirits," you said.

"I don't think it will last very long," I said.

...

We decided to skip work and have a day where we just stayed in bed and talked about things. Sometimes you think you don't have anything to talk about with me, but all you have to do is turn off the TV and the Internet and we find other ways to fill the silence. The slow time.

The blinds weren't shut all the way, and the sun flickered through, sometimes lighting us up and sometimes going dark. There must have been clouds passing by. "I feel like I'm on LSD," you said. You told me that you had taken three pills for anxiety. I can never remember what they're called. "I really am a pill popper," you said. "It's just part of my makeup."

We took turns picking out CDs to listen to and talking about ex-lovers from before we met. I caught myself rambling on about one woman whom I didn't even have much in common with. I suddenly felt dumb while I spoke of her, but I wanted to finish the story. I wanted you to hear the end of it (about how the woman moved to Alaska and gave me a fake phone number that I dialed repeatedly for six months).

Then you talked about the one lover that you never thought you'd be able to let go of. You actually had an old letter stashed away somewhere and you found it and read it to me. "Just so you know he was worthwhile," you said. You started reading the whole letter, and it was long. There was a stream-of-consciousness style to it that I appreciated but sometimes felt lost in. I wanted to stop you but I didn't. I felt like I had to absorb this other guy's feelings, and then I would better understand you. But I also felt like that was a previous version of you, and I didn't want to understand it. I have a new version of you, I thought to myself.

Later in the afternoon, before the kids got home from school, we went for a walk. We stopped for coffee at an espresso cart. I joked with the barista and asked him if he could make a heart with the foam on my mocha, and he said he would try. He said he could do hearts sometimes or he could do apples.

"There's not much difference between a heart and an apple," you said to me as we walked away.

"An apple is just a fucked-up heart," I said.

We stopped at a park and you swung on a swing. "I get nauseous doing this," you told me. But you were swinging really high, and I was trying to look up your dress.

Before we started back home, you said, "I want us to write love notes for each other."

We sat by a fountain and you looked for paper and pens. You had two pens but nothing to write on.

We decided to write on our paper cups. I turned mine carefully as I tried to write neatly, my shaky letters spelling out the story of a recent good day with you. You watched over my shoulder for a while and I told you not to look. You wrote something for me too, but your handwriting was much neater.

We traded cups at the end. We read them and laughed. We toasted. We drank. We brought them home and kept them.

...

I still keep all the notes you've written for me. Scraps of papers you slipped in my coat pocket with sweet words and dirty promises. Letters you mailed to me whenever we were apart. Birthday, Valentine's, Christmas cards—some handmade and some store-bought.

I also have the nightgown you wore those first nights we were together, the one that looks like it could have belonged to your grandmother. It's the color of cloudy lace, with blue and red flowers embroidered on it. A little tattered around the hem, by your left knee. You tried to throw it away, but I wanted to keep it. I put it in a box with other keepsakes. You found it and tried to throw it away again. I hid it from you better the second time.

I have things from other girlfriends too—photos, letters, a guitar, a thermos from a camping trip, an old suit that doesn't fit me anymore, a stack of poems stapled in the corner.

Once, in my twenties, I was moving and I threw out a box of souvenirs from my high school girlfriends. I regret that now. I sometimes wish I could go up to the attic and rummage through a box and randomly come across a close-up shot of Andrea's puckered lips coming at me—a blurry reminder that someone loved me even in my crudest hormonal phase. There were several letters from a sophomore girl named Mandy, all of them soaked in her mom's perfume. I don't remember her voice or her eyes or what we talked about. But I remembered the way she smelled riding home in my car with me. That's past tense now: *remembered.*

We're at the age when we start to forget things from our lives. You're worse than I am—you don't even remember all your boyfriends' names. That's why I want to store my things away, keep them where I can find them. The good stuff for sure. Sometimes even the broken stuff. There's a lot of that around too. I can't bring myself to throw it out. I always think to myself: *I'll fix that someday.*

The other week, I found a large hourglass that you bought for me when we were in Florida. It was originally about a foot high, filled with dark sand. We had it shipped home and it arrived broken. I'm not sure what I was planning to do with it, but I put it in the attic right away, like it might mend itself alongside the other memories up there. But it was still just shards of glass and sand in the box we shipped it in. I was tempted to run my fingers through it.

. . .

We watched an old TV show from the nineties and chuckled at the jokes we'd heard before, but underneath our familiar laugh track there was an unsettling déjà vu. I used to watch this show with my ex-wife and you used to watch it with your ex-husband. This kind of unintentional nostalgia started to poison the air around us by the third commercial break. We couldn't figure out why we felt like shit when we got in bed.

An hour later, we were out of bed, putting on our shoes. We walked around our neighborhood, then the next one, and then the one after that. We looked through people's windows to see what they were watching. We searched the sky for UFOs or comets. We started jogging and then cutting through yards, stealing flowers. We sprinted down the middle of the streets. We wanted to sweat this out.

...

We tried to incorporate food into our sex. Whipped cream was an obvious choice, and we used up a whole can of it in a couple of nights.

We played with chocolate syrup, but only in small doses. You didn't want to get the sheets messy, but you tolerated my enthusiasm.

Then we tried using honey, but it was too sticky and uncomfortable. "It's fucking up my trim," you said.

I rolled off of you, licking my fingers. I wondered if we really had to do something different to keep our sex life exciting. Maybe we could try bondage or some kind of kink, but that would feel fake. Still, would it hurt to try something different? It's funny how self-conscious we became about making mistakes.

...

You don't like the expression *head of hair*.

"It sounds like a skull with a wig inside of it," you once said.

Maxine was parading around the apartment one day with a pink wig on, saying, "How do you like my head of hair?"

"Stop saying that," you told her. "It makes me think of the word *skull*, and *skull* makes me think of death."

"I wonder what it feels like to be dead," said Maxine innocently.

"You're twelve years old," you said. "You won't be dead for another hundred years."

Maxine stopped and frowned. "I'll have to wait so long," she said.

You kissed her on the chin and said, "Life is good. You'll have a good life all the way to the end. I just know it."

Later on, you felt bad and told me you said it all wrong. I told you that it was fine, and that you were a sweet and beautiful mom. You cried yourself to sleep.

...

That Halloween, the kids had two neighborhood friends over and we dressed the four of them up in different-colored sheets with eyeholes cut out so they could see. They were the ghosts from the Pac-Man game. You and I wore big bulky cardboard costumes painted yellow. Yours had a red bow on top and lipstick painted around the mouth. We were Pac-Man and Ms. Pac-Man.

At the end of the night, after the other kids went home, Vince seemed sad. "This will probably be the last Halloween I go out for. I'm going to be too old next year," he said.

"You're never too old," I said stupidly.

"But I'm getting too old for a lot of stuff," said Vince. "All of my stuffed animals are in the basement. I think Hot Wheels are stupid now, but I used to think they were so cool. And I want to get rid of my *Star Wars* posters. Roberto has posters of rated-R movies on his wall."

I popped some M&M's into my mouth and put my hand on his knee. "It's okay," I said. "That's just part of life. Even when you grow up, you go through phases of liking new things and getting bored of old stuff. I just realized last year that I don't like the Beatles anymore. And I used to think army boots looked good on women, but now I'm kind of scared of that."

Vince spread a handful of candy corn on the table in front of us and made it into the shape of a heart. "Remember last year when we watched *Sleeping Beauty* on Halloween?" he asked. He paused for a moment but didn't look at me for an answer. "I've probably watched that movie like thirty times."

"Probably more like two hundred," I corrected him.

"Yeah, maybe," he said. "But that's the last time. I mean, I didn't know it when we were watching it, but I don't think I want to see it again. For a long time I was scared of the witch but now I don't really care. Does that mean I'm growing up?"

"Sure," I said. "That's a good thing. You used to be scared of *Scooby-Doo* and the 'Thriller' video too, but now you can watch more mature movies with us." I thought about that phrase for a second: *mature movies.*

It was weird to see Vince feeling contemplative and nostalgic. I thought about the other Disney movies that we could finally pack up and move to the basement, along with some of the dustier toys taking up room in his closet. He was a little hoarder who never threw anything out. I decided I'd wait a few days and round that stuff up while he was at school. I'd take it to the basement or donate it to Goodwill and hope he didn't notice the parts of his past disappearing. It was like a graveyard down there, underneath us.

. . .

That Christmas felt different, maybe because Vince and Maxine were less excited about it. Instead of asking for numerous things like they had in years past, they had a hard time thinking of one thing. Like they were too cool to ask now. And since they were getting older, it was hard to guess what they might like—so many things could be seen as "too young" or "too old" for them.

We let them open one present each on Christmas Eve and we watched their faces to gauge their reactions. Maxine got a makeup kit from your aunt in Missouri and seemed happy about that. Vince got a pair of racquetball rackets from your brother. He looked confused at first—his expression asked: *When did I ask for these?*—but then he realized that we would have to get a membership to a gym with courts and he became excited by the idea of that.

On Christmas morning, you opened your present from me—a new camera—and started testing it out. We figured out the timer and took photos of all of us together. We stood in front of the tree, arms around each other, like an ordinary family. I secretly thought of those photos as presents to myself.

# YEAR FOUR

I sat on the couch and watched the cat cleaning himself.

Sometimes he sat and watched me take a shower.

One day, the cat and I watched you take a shower. Your hands were so graceful. Slow motion. It's so interesting to see how we clean ourselves in this world.

...

Sometimes I wanted to talk to you for a long time, like kids staying up all night, going on about the smallest things. I loved how your voice got hoarse after a few drinks or a few hours. I wondered what you'd sound like as an old lady.

I admit that I occasionally drifted off when you talked and I got lost in the sound of your voice instead of the words. But you'd pause at just the right moment and say something strange and crazy and wonderful. Something I'd never heard anyone say. Like the time you said, "I want to wear you like a bear suit."

I would even call your phone to hear your voice talking on the outgoing message—the cute way you said *thank you* at the end.

...

One time I came home and found a bunch of broken dishes in the sink. Some pieces of them were on the counter and kitchen floor as well. You were having a bad day and wanted to see what it would be like to shatter something. I found you in the bedroom, crying. You were wearing some kind of goggles or protective eyewear. I was glad you'd taken some precautions before having your fit. You told me you were up-set because Maxine had flunked a class and then used your credit card without telling you. And you had also gotten your hair done that morning and thought it turned out horrible. And then you got in trouble at the library for someone else's mistake. And then you burned the chicken we were going to have for dinner and the car battery was dead.

"Feel better now?" I asked you.

"Will you clean up my mess, please?" you asked me.

I went back into the kitchen, swept up and gathered the pieces and slivers as much as I could. You came up behind me and held me hard. Your hands gripped my shirt and a couple of buttons popped open.

"Don't walk around in here with bare feet for a while," I said.

"Will you do everything else around here for the rest of the day, please?" you asked. "I still have some shitty feelings inside."

I told you I'd take care of everything and make it good as new eventually. You leaned over the kitchen sink like you were going to throw up into it or scream down its pipes. I watched you and waited, but nothing happened.

...

Vince came home from school with something dangling from his right ear. He slipped by quickly, like he was trying to hide something.

"What's that?" I said.

"Nothing," he said.

I went to his bedroom but the door was closed. I knocked before opening it a crack. He was on his bed, pretending to get his homework out. He had a hat on, although he never wore hats. "Let me see," I said as good-naturedly as I could. He moved his head so I couldn't see. I laughed, and he laughed back nervously. I saw the earring. The expression on his face was trying to tell me it was no big deal. He was still rustling through his school folders.

"A lightning bolt?" I said. "I thought you were supposed to start with a stud. Where did you do this?"

"I got it with Roberto. He got both ears pierced."

I put my hand on his shoulder to assure him that I wasn't mad, but I wondered if he knew the difference between having his left or right ear pierced. "Why did you do that side?" I asked him.

"Because my hair is parted on that side and it looks better that way," he said. He thought about it for a few seconds and probably figured out what I was thinking. "It doesn't mean anything," he said. "This isn't the 1980s."

I wanted to be cool about it, but I did feel something, like a sort of left-out-ness. I looked over to the corner of his room and saw a stuffed animal that we'd won at a carnival about five years before. I had knocked over some stacked-up cans and won it for him. We named it Carnival Bear, and when we got home that day, he had to introduce Carnival Bear to the rest of his stuffed animals. I remember Vince's little voice introducing the "family."

I looked at Vince's lightning bolt. It looked like something I would have wanted in my ear when I was a kid.

...

Our neighbors from across the street came over to say hello while you and I were sitting on the porch. This seemed weird at first, since we didn't ever talk to them. They were about our age, maybe a little younger, but they had old-people names like Marge and Cecil. We would see their kid playing by himself in their front yard a lot. We invited them to sit in the two empty lawn chairs. We formed an uncomfortable circle.

"We feel like we should tell you about something your son said to our boy," Marge said, looking at you. You looked at me as if hoping her gaze would follow. I could tell it wasn't going to be good.

I cleared my throat and said, "What is it?"

Marge's mouth snapped tight and Cecil spoke this time. "He told our son, Clyde, that there was a new candy bar that he should ask his mother for."

My stomach dropped. I knew what was coming next.

Cecil lowered his voice and whispered, with a mix of anger and embarrassment, "He told Clyde that it was called a BJ."

I sat there, pokerfaced.

"He asked his own mother," Cecil started to say, and then turned his head.

"He asked *me* for a BJ," Marge said. It seemed strange that she emphasized the word *me*.

"I am so sorry about that," I said. "I will definitely have a talk with him." I stammered some more apologies and then awkwardly transitioned to some softer small talk. I was laughing a little in my head though, recalling how I had done the exact same thing to a younger neighbor kid when I was twelve. And how I'd told the story about it just the week before, when I was getting drunk at our friend's barbecue. Vince was playing croquet nearby, but I knew now that he was also enjoying my loud, loose tongue. The bad gags of delinquent youth. Sometimes it's hard to stop them from bleeding over into the next generation.

. . .

Something happened with your brother that I never told you about. We were out having drinks and he asked me if I'd ever been with a man. I told him I had a few times, but I preferred women. He asked me about my experiences, and then asked me how it was with you. He can sometimes look a lot like you, so it was especially odd to talk to him about this. I changed the subject.

When we were driving home, he unzipped his pants and pulled his cock out quietly, so that I wouldn't notice. He grabbed my hand and tried to put it there but I pulled away. "What do you think you're doing?" I said. I didn't tell him to put himself away or say anything else.

"I just wanted to show you," he said. He was stroking it slowly. We drove around a block of shops and restaurants and I wondered if anyone else could see what he was doing.

"You're going to get us in trouble, Daniel," I said, turning the car onto a darker side street.

He told me to pull over, and I did. I turned and watched him. His face was like yours, but different. He asked me if I liked to watch your face when you came. He asked me how often we had sex. He asked me if you gave good head. He said, "Put your mouth on it like she does."

I told him no, and then he asked if I wanted to see him come. I said yes, and he kept going. He lifted his shirt a little, and I saw his cock pulse and ejaculate on his belly. It was all over his hand. He found a napkin in the glove box and delicately wiped himself up. "Can I watch you now?" he asked.

"I don't think I can," I said, though I probably could have. I felt myself becoming coy for his benefit.

He reached over and put his hand between my legs. "I'll be ready whenever you are," he said.

. . .

One of my friends knew I needed extra money, so he got me a side job at a women's health club. I helped out with their self-defense classes. I had to be the guy in the big padded suit that the women released their suffocated rage on. But before that could happen, the instructor—a military-looking woman with one of the biggest and strongest asses I'd ever seen—ran through several scenarios of would-be attack. Everything she said started calm but ramped up into a shouted series of slogans about self-preservation and empowerment. I found myself getting worked up by her words as well. When the time came to lumber out onto the wrestling mats, I wanted myself to be the rod that their lightning smacked.

I did this job for twenty classes. The first hit was always the worst, maybe because of the pretend scenario. I was to approach the instructor from behind, ready to grope her like a creep. Just as my padded hands inched hotly to her ass, she would turn slightly and smash the side of my oversize head with her elbow. Then she would turn and give me a swift kick between my legs, while screaming, "No! Stop!" Or sometimes she would just yell a guttural and beast-like noise, something between a scream and a sickening retch.

When it was the students' turns, I enjoyed it more. Their hits, screams, and kicks were sloppier and usually weaker, and didn't hurt as much in the suit. I felt like I was in a protective shell, like a turtle made of thick foam. My head was covered by a giant orange bell-shaped helmet that smelled terrible by the end of class.

I talked to you about these classes and even urged you to take one. I found myself being transformed by the experience. I was proud to be part of this process where so many women would learn how to take care of unwanted attention, and I would sometimes exaggerate my pain or my tumbles like a professional wrestler. But I also found myself slipping into the head of an attacker more and more. I wanted to find some new maneuver that might allow me actually to get a feel of the instructor's ass. I think she would have given me a playful but competitive nod after class and said, "You got me that time, but watch out tomorrow."

On my last class as the attacker, you signed up without telling me. When the instructor called me out, I waddled from the locker room and saw your face, looking slightly nauseated or scared. But when it was eventually your turn to defend yourself from me, you did so admirably.

You beat the shit out of me like a pro. It was like you forgot I was in that suit, like it really was someone else, maybe someone from your past, who did something to you that you couldn't erase. I was on the mat and you were standing over me, screaming, "No!" I thought I saw steam or smoke rising out of you. Some kind of ghost floating out of the back of your head.

. . .

One morning, you showed me an obituary for a woman named Cynthia who had died at the age of fifty-two. It didn't say how she had died, though. It listed a funeral service in two days and said she had "lived a rich life that was full of loving friends and valuable work for her community." There was a list of relatives who were still alive, including a daughter and her own mother. Two ex-husbands had also survived her.

"My father had an affair with this woman," you told me. You were frozen in front of me, like you weren't sure what to do with yourself. A kettle of hot water started whistling loudly on the stove behind you. I got up to take it off the hot element. I asked if you were okay.

"I don't know," you said. "It's just unsettling to think about now. I met her once, but it always stuck with me in a strange way."

I looked at the photo next to the woman's obituary. It looked like it had been taken when she was in her thirties. She was wearing jeans and a fuzzy-looking white sweater. She had long, straight blonde hair and was slim and tall, like she could have been a model. But her smile looked odd, like she wasn't used to holding her mouth that way. "What happened?" I asked you.

You poured hot water into a cup with lemon and honey and looked at the steam rising from it as you gathered your memories. "My dad was on some kind of committee or board or something. It was a charity thing, and Cynthia was part of it too. He had meetings every week, or so he said. I was in sixth grade. I remember that because I hated sixth grade and my father was never around to help me. We had a party one night at our house, and I had to walk around with trays of different kinds of hors d'oeuvres. It was fun at first, but I got bored pretty fast. I met Cynthia and thought she was really pretty. She had a cute hat that she let me wear. It was like a Chanel hat and I thought she was probably rich so she might let me keep it. My mom saw me walking around with it though and she made me give it back. I looked around for Cynthia to give the hat back and saw her and my dad, alone in the kitchen. She was leaning over to grab something out of our cupboard and dad grabbed her ass and squeezed it. I'm sure this happened really fast, but to me it was like he had really felt her up for a long time."

Your voice cracked when you said "long time," but then you laughed a little and continued. "She stood up and playfully slapped his butt back and they almost started wrestling. I think they were a little drunk. I hid behind the door so they couldn't see me. I heard my dad say, in a weird quiet voice, 'I'll get you later, on the drive home.' I hadn't heard his voice sound like that before. I made some loud stepping noises so they could hear me and then I came into the kitchen. They took a step back from each other, and I handed the hat back to Cynthia. I felt this rush of heat go through me and I said, 'I don't want this anymore.' She took it from me and smiled, just like the smile in this picture."

We both looked at the photo in the newspaper. You pointed at the date and address for the funeral service. "Let's go to this," you said.

...

There was a strip of photos that we had hidden somewhere. Four pictures of us from a photo booth when we still had other people's rings on our fingers. You could see them in one of the poses. We never thought to take them off.

We thought that people would just think that we were married to each other when we were out somewhere—that I had given you your ring and you had given me my ring.

We were good at pretending to be one strong couple, not a combination of two weak ones. But I do remember that time at the dessert shop when you pointed at something excitedly and accidentally called me by your husband's name. You didn't notice your mistake, and I just rolled with it, like nothing happened.

There is no sign of rings in any other photo of us.

. . .

I'd always thought that going to a stranger's funeral would be interesting. One of the first movies we saw together was *Harold and Maude* and we both loved how Harold's hobby was going to funerals. But going to Cynthia's funeral was different, of course. There could have been people there who knew you. It had been about twenty years since you last saw her. The closer we get to forty, the less time twenty years seems.

We sat in one of the last pews of the church and tried to figure out who her ex-husbands were. We were nervous about people talking to us, but we made up a story in case anyone did. We knew that she had a lot of money somehow and had donated to charities, so we would say that we worked for a homeless shelter. But no one spoke to us.

There was a slide show of photographs that faded in and out on a screen next to her casket: Cynthia holding a small dog and laughing as it licked her face . . . Cynthia eating a giant slice of pizza . . . Cynthia posing with political figures, mayors and first ladies . . . Cynthia holding a giant pair of scissors, ready to cut the ribbon on a new building . . . Cynthia and her daughter wearing matching designer dresses . . . Cynthia and her friends holding glasses of wine and smiling at a birthday party.

Some swelling, sentimental music that sounded like Muzak floated in the air. You nudged me and pointed to the organ player in the balcony. I watched him swaying dramatically to the sounds coming out of the giant instrument. I looked down at my polished black shoes and tried not to laugh. I noticed that you were shrinking beside me and I wondered if something was bothering you. You squeezed my arm hard and pointed back up to the balcony. When I looked again, I saw that the organ player was your dad.

. . .

Cynthia's memorial service lasted more than two hours. After we saw your dad playing the organ, we moved to the back of the church where he wouldn't be able to see us, though we still heard the swelling hum of the instrument fade in and out between each eulogist. One after the other, they talked about her generosity as a philanthropist, the amount of time she'd spent supporting local school programs, her strong political beliefs, and even the occasional editorial that she had written for the newspaper.

You kept looking behind us, as if your dad was going to walk by and approach the altar himself. I guess it wasn't out of the question. You did say their affair lasted for five years.

Cynthia's daughter was the last speaker of the memorial and she looked like a younger version of her mother. She was a model and painter, probably around twenty years old. She could barely speak, she was crying so hard. If the whole church wasn't crying before, they were now. Even we cried, and we couldn't understand anything she was saying.

...

You were a freshman in high school when your mom found out about your father's affair. You came home to them throwing things at each other in the living room. At first, you thought they were playing because they were throwing pillows and couch cushions, but then books and plants and framed photos were flying and crashing everywhere. "Five years!" your mom kept shouting, and you didn't know what they were fighting about. You yelled at them to stop. Your mom told your dad to get out, and then she shook her head and said, "No no no. You're staying here and I'll leave. Because I know where you'll go if you leave." You told me about how the room froze for a moment then and you noticed they both had blood running down their faces, as if they had each smashed something over the other's head.

...

You and your mom moved out for several months after she found out about the affair, reluctantly giving your dad time to figure things out. You spent weekends with him during that time. You told me about a day when your dad took you out to the beach and tried to have a real one-on-one conversation with you about the situation. You told me that he could hardly talk because he kept sobbing, and sometimes someone would walk by, even though you were on the far end of the beach. "There are two good women who are in love with me, and I'm in love with both of them," he told you. It was like he was trying to ask for your advice. You told me he couldn't look you in the eyes.

You and your mom moved back in with him before Christmas that year. You described the mood around the house as stilted, as if your mom and dad were two actors trying to re-enact what it was like when they were happy together. That's when you started taking pills, you told me. Mostly painkillers and Ritalin from a rich kid in your honors English class.

You were never sure if your dad stopped seeing Cynthia. You once heard your brother say that they got back in touch after your mother died a few years later.

. . .

Sometimes I called you when you were still with your husband. I could tell if he was around by the tone in your voice. If you were alone, I could hear a warmth, a kind of purr in your words. If he was with you, you'd sound more guarded. All business. But I was still happy just to hear your voice. I'd say "I love you" at the end of the call and you'd say, "Okay. Bye."

. . .

Your brother told me a story about an affair he once had with a married man. Daniel would buy the man gifts and write him notes, and the man had to hide them from his wife. Some of the gifts were things the man could not take home, so Daniel had to keep them at his place. But the man hardly came over, so after a while it seemed like Daniel was buying himself gifts. There was a shelf full of things meant for this man: a framed photo of them together, a poem written by Daniel, a coffee-table book of erotic art inscribed to the man, a bracelet, a two-hundred-dollar bottle of wine, a G.I. Joe action figure that they'd joked about at a vintage store, and several mix CDs of songs about love and sex.

"Instead of being with this man, I would be with his things," Daniel told me. "You're lucky you don't have to hide anything like that."

I thought about my night in the car with him, and wondered if I really was lucky and if I had nothing to hide.

"Did it make the gifts seem less sweet?" I asked him.

"It did," he said. "They started to feel like unreal objects. Like pretend things in a ghost world. Like a museum that no one is allowed to see."

I thought Daniel was right, but I felt bad for the man. I empathized with his position—perhaps more than Daniel's for some reason. I dwelled on the thing Daniel said about the gifts seeming like a museum. But I changed it a little, maybe to make their situation less sad. I thought: *Every person is a museum. Everyone is a museum.*

. . .

We tried to structure some new activities that would become learning tools for the kids. We would write a famous quote and some historical facts about upcoming dates on a dry-erase board in the kitchen and we would talk about them while eating dinner. If the kids had their own quotes or facts, they could write them on the board as well.

We did that for five weeks before the kids seemed bored with it. They stopped looking at the board and never wrote on it. (Right next to the refrigerator may not have been the best place.)

I think we lost interest in this exercise too. We stopped writing on the board. I wondered if the kids noticed this and realized that we gave up on it. Moms and dads get bored too. Moms and dads get busy. Moms and dads run out of ideas. Moms and dads get tired.

...

Around the same time, I could tell that the kids were getting bored of us. They didn't seem to enjoy our company anymore. They wouldn't even pretend to be interested in what we talked about.

"You guys aren't even eighteen yet," I said one day. "You're not old enough to move out and survive on your own." I tried to put enough anger in my voice to get their attention.

It seemed like Vince and Maxine regarded us as uncool now, and in some ways that hurt more than their simple boredom with us. We would show them videos of bands we liked and they would just walk away before the second verse.

...

When I was about nine years old, my family—Mom, Dad, and my older brother—went on a vacation to Japan. It was such a different experience to me that I didn't understand anything we were doing, and I struggled to enjoy even the simplest activities—things I felt would have been more fun in an English-speaking place.

My mom and dad ate it up though, and used their new Super 8 camera to shoot hours of footage.

The day after we returned home, my dad excitedly transferred some of the highlights onto videotape and invited a bunch of friends and relatives over for a vacation video party. After everyone ate Japanese food and drank sake, we all gathered around the big television and hit play on the VCR. The vacation footage began midsentence and my dad said, "Oops, gotta rewind it a little." The machine whirred and made a clunking sound and he hit play again. The screen fluttered with static for a moment and then about three seconds of a strange image: a woman stroking a man's enormous penis while he lay on a bed.

The room got immediately silent. Then an image of our family standing in front of a giant Buddha statue appeared, and my dad's voice started narrating on the tape. "Hello and welcome to *Good Times in Japan*, our very own family vacation diary."

Fifteen minutes into it, my mom got up and left the room crying.

The next day, I found the tape and played the part again. I watched it over and over again, the woman's hand going up and down. I couldn't figure out what was happening or what could possibly happen next.

. . .

We were in the bar of the hotel after I got off work one night. Our heads felt lopsided with sloshed alcohol. The DJ played songs from the eighties and our friends said they wanted to dance. I flailed my arms like a joke and grinned like an idiot. I did not mean to act so silly and I quickly became silent. A gloom settled over me as I realized that I did not know how to dance anymore. It had been ten years since I last danced. Ten static and dance-free years. I looked at my hands and my feet reluctantly. They were dead people.

...

Vince didn't even want to be seen with us sometimes.

We'd go to a café and he'd sit at another table.

We'd go to Target and he would hang out in the electronics section the whole time. Sometimes I wondered if the employees thought he was a shoplifter.

If I tried to show affection, a sort of parental gesture like putting my hand on his shoulder, when there were other kids around, he would shrug me off. He'd flash me a mean look. A face that I thought only a hurt lover could make.

...

The host of the radio advice show always tells people that threesomes will destroy their relationship. But I think the one we had with Janelle made us stronger.

It began when I met Janelle at a party and started holding hands with her under the table.

Then Janelle and I started talking to each other a lot over the phone.

Then all three of us went out for drinks.

Then we went back to her small apartment.

When I went to the bathroom, you began making out with Janelle in her bedroom. I waited several minutes before coming in and sitting next to the two of you. I asked if we could all kiss. Hands, shoulders, and hair. We rubbed through clothes and buttons and zippers. Two hours later, when you stood up and straightened yourself out, Janelle whispered harshly to me, "I did that for you."

We stayed friends with Janelle for a year or so, but we never really grew to love her. She eventually moved away without telling us.

...

One of the guys you worked with was named Jon, and I knew he had a thing for you. You went out to lunch with him all the time. When we were separated, you went out on a date with him, even though you insisted it wasn't a date. You went to dinner and then to a play. He also gave you a silver watch with an engraving on the back. It said, *Make time for us. J.*

You didn't tell me about it, but I saw it one night when I was snooping around. I rifled through your dresser while you were in the shower. You wore the watch a few days later and said it was from a girlfriend who didn't want it anymore. I looked at it like I was seeing it for the first time. You watched me nervously as I squinted at the inscription. But it had been scratched off now. "Why is it all scratched up?" I asked.

You shrugged and said, "I don't know. Maybe it was personal."

. . .

You started to think I was falling out of love with you. You said I didn't share things with you anymore. I asked you what you meant and you said I hadn't read out loud to you in months. And you said I didn't take your picture anymore. I didn't come in to put more hot water in when you took a bath. I didn't put lemon in your tap water anymore. I didn't pick up your shoes when it was time for bed like I used to. You said I said *no* more often. I didn't even push the cart at the grocery store when we went together. You said my hands felt cold. You said my lips didn't open so easily. You said I was not all here. And I asked you, "Where?"

. . .

We went to a cheap motel room once to work out our problems. It was less expensive than a payment to our couples counselor and more private than trying to do it at the hotel where I worked.

We made an agreement to stay in the room together and talk for at least two hours. We were not supposed to touch each other.

Two hours later, we were covered in sweat and we had set off the fire alarm somehow.

"I can't have therapy if your hands are all over me," you said.

"It's physical therapy," I said.

"You always have the right answer," you said.

...

We were lying in bed and I was walking the fingers of my right hand up your legs, closer and closer to your ass. Then I placed my hand flat and imagined it was a surfboard. When it hit the curve of your ass, it was like hitting a beautiful wave. I did it quickly a few times. I did it in slow motion. You didn't say anything. In fact, you were asleep. You started to snore a little. It sounded like the low hum of a motorcycle. I thought of my hand as a motorcycle. Your ass was a ramp. I was a daredevil, airborne.

...

You told me that the worst physical pain you'd ever been in was that one time, a few years ago, when you got a really bad sunburn. You'd called in sick to work so you could spend the day on the beach while I stayed home and watched the kids.

In the middle of the afternoon, you fell asleep for two hours in the sand. Your skin already looked tough and leathery when you got home and you begged me to put some kind of salve or balm on your back.

You rifled through the medicine cabinet and found some lotion. I squeezed some out of the tube and spread it all over your back. A couple of minutes later, you were writhing on the couch. It was getting worse, you said. It burned, you said. You tore your clothes off and jumped in the shower. You turned on the cold water and let it run over your back. "Damn it!" you shouted. "It's fucking burning!"

I didn't know what to do. I looked at the tube of lotion and realized it was not meant to treat sunburns. One of the ingredients was alcohol.

"I can't even take a shower," you said. "The water hurts." You were starting to cry. I brought you a towel and you told me to put it on you slowly. I rested it softly on your shoulders but you screamed and collapsed to the floor. I brought in an electric fan and let it blow on your back as you squirmed around more and said, "Okay okay okay. Please get better. Okay okay okay. I feel like I'm on fire!"

About an hour later, you finally got up and started putting on your clothes. "I have to get out of here," you said. "I have to distract myself and drive somewhere." You said you wanted to be alone.

You went to a club called Satyricon, and they were hosting a cabaret show. You started drinking quickly, in hopes that it would numb the pain. You couldn't stay still and you paced around the place like a shark circling in a tank. One of your old boyfriends was there and you talked to him. He thought it was funny that you had to walk around like you were doing, sometimes shrugging your shoulders and arching your back to combat the burning and itching. You were still hurting, but you let him joke about it with you.

After a few drinks, the itching felt more like a soft vibration going through your body and you felt like you needed to shed your skin like a snake. "I want to show you something," you said to the old boyfriend. You went to a small secret upstairs room that one of your friends showed you once. You took off your shirt and showed the old boyfriend your burn.

The blisters had already started. "Don't laugh," you said.

He didn't laugh. He looked at your skin closely. He put his hands on you. He squeezed. You told me later how much it really hurt.

. . .

I know you liked it when I openly wept without trying to hide it. Like when we watched *E.T.* when the kids were younger, or when I read that newspaper story about the seeing-eye dogs. You turned your head to me, reached over, and dabbed my cheeks with your sleeve. I smelled your wrist and kissed it. You didn't make fun of me for any of that.

You once said to me, "I like that you like to cry. I love that you love to love."

. . .

Vince said he and his best friend, Roberto, were doing "movie life" now. I didn't know what he meant, so he explained to me that it's when you imagine that your life is a movie.

"I used to pretend a camera was always on me and I had to act cool or interesting," he said. "Then I noticed that there really are cameras everywhere."

I wondered if this could be a precursor to paranoia or mistrust of the government.

"One of our teachers said there used to *not* be cameras everywhere. And then Roberto told me that he also thinks about movie life."

"I did that sometimes too. Pretended like I was in a movie," I told him. "But you're not really on TV, so you should just act natural. All those traffic cameras and cameras at your school and at the mall and on buses are just for security."

"So I should just ignore the cameras?" Vince asked.

"Well, you shouldn't always act like you're being broadcast on a reality TV show," I said. I smiled a little but then worried that I was being condescending.

"The weird thing is that when I don't act like I'm on TV, I feel kind of sad or something," he said. "Like my show has been cancelled."

...

We went for a long walk with the kids. It was a beautiful spring day and I sometimes put my hand on your ass when Vince and Maxine ran ahead of us. I liked to feel it move against my hand, the soft red fabric of your skirt. I didn't squeeze or push. I just touched and looked, catching glimpses of your legs. The muscles in your calves. Your sharp ankles. I found myself getting aroused, and I whispered in your ear, "I think I'm going to have to fuck your brains out when we get home."

You brushed your hand against my crotch to see if I was serious.

When we got home fifteen minutes later, we saw that the neighbors were having a yard sale and the kids wanted to look. I pulled the last six dollars out of my wallet and gave the money to Vince. "You two can buy whatever you can get for this, as long as you agree about it," I told him. He nodded. "Okay. See you at home," I said. "Take your time."

Then you and I quickly ran into the apartment. We thought about going into the bedroom, but we didn't want the kids charging in five minutes later wanting to show us what they bought. We went to the kitchen, where we could see the neighbors' yard sale from the window. You slipped your panties off and I unbuttoned my shorts. You lifted your skirt and placed your hands flat on the counter next to the kitchen sink. We kept our eyes on the kids as we did it. They were looking at a table of knickknacks. Things made out of seashells and driftwood. If they had looked over to the window, they would've seen our blissful faces looking out, our eyes half closed and drifting, barely keeping them in focus.

I had my hands on your waist, lifting you just slightly.

I looked outside and saw Vince holding a giant textbook of some kind. He opened it up and smelled the pages. He put it back down.

"You're going to make me come," you said. "I'm gonna come in the fucking kitchen." You reached over and turned the kitchen sink on full blast. You started moaning and your head fell forward. Steam started to rise and I caught Maxine looking toward us. I saw her say something to Vince and then I lost her in the steam.

You started moving aggressively against me, grinding in circles. I held you tighter and focused on your back and shoulders. I wanted to lean down and lick along your shoulder blades, but we were convulsing and I thought you might knock one of my teeth out. (One time you almost broke my nose this way.)

My right hand moved up and cupped your breast. I thought about biting the nape of your neck. I thought about putting you on the dinner table. I thought about fucking you on the tiled floor. But I just put my forehead down in the middle of your back and came inside you.

We stayed that way for a minute, waiting for our breathing to slow down and our composure to return. You reached over and turned the sink off. When the steam cleared we saw that the kids were not there. But as we cleaned up after ourselves, the front door opened and their excited chatter filled the air.

...

We were sitting on the couch with the nightly news on the TV. You were flipping through a science magazine, and I was clipping my fingernails. The beautiful black weather lady came on and I watched her gesture elegantly with her long arms at the storm front coming down from Canada. She was wearing a tight red dress that squeezed around her knees and made her look taller than usual.

"Sheila Young looks really good tonight," I said.

"Oh yeah," you said. You lowered the magazine from your face to get a look. You looked at me and tried to gauge the level of fantasizing in my head. "What do you like about her?" you asked.

"She's sleek," I said. "She looks like she's lost some weight or something."

"How much weight do you think?"

"I don't know, maybe fifteen pounds."

"I lost fifteen pounds this year too," you said. "Thanks for noticing."

There was a long silence. I watched the Doppler radar swirling behind Sheila Young's fine figure, as if it were coming out of her backside. I imagined you there instead, in front of the green screen, pointing at warm fronts, temperatures, and humidity levels. I saw you become a sexy black weather lady.

"You look really good too," I said.

. . .

I was bothered by the thought of an ex-girlfriend. Someone I hadn't thought about in several years. I called her and she answered, not knowing who it was.

"It's me," I said nervously. She wanted to know why I called, and I said, "I don't know." She asked if I had something to say. I said, "I'm sorry," because it seemed like the only way to start.

"Why are you sorry?" she asked me.

"Because I realize now that I ruined your life," I answered.

"How do you think you ruined my life?" she said. Every conversation we'd had was like this, and that was one of the reasons I became exhausted by her and broke up with her. They were long, circular conversations. She was all intellect and no instinct. But I didn't realize this until the last days of our whirlwind relationship.

I made promises to her that I didn't keep. I unveiled romantic plans before I thought about them realistically. She said she loved me more than she should.

We were young, still in college, and she was part of a well-off family that strived to control her. She was supposed to become a lawyer. Seeing me was not permitted for some reason. She wanted to obey her parents, but I would practically beg her to defy them, to spend as much time with me as possible. We saw each other for six months, mostly discreet dates and sleepovers, before breaking up. She was pregnant, though, and didn't tell me. She was in denial about it until she started showing.

Her parents found out, and she was sent away to have the baby secretly, with some relatives in Canada. The baby was put up for adoption and her parents disowned her. She started drinking and couldn't keep a job. I didn't hear about the baby until after the fact, but I felt responsible for how her life imploded. She couldn't quite talk to me about it then. We tried a few times, but she'd always end up breaking down and she'd tell me to stay away. I was clueless for a while though, and I would try to reconnect with her and send her little gifts. I didn't know why it was so hard for her to hear from me, just be friends. I didn't know how she could love me as much as she insisted she did but also regret that love and want to be left alone.

But it eventually sank in. That was sixteen years ago, and I finally realized that she never recovered. When I broke up with her, it was sudden, and then I was with Sheryl, who became my wife, and the mother of my son. I just went on with my selfish life.

I never thought about that baby much either, though I knew it was a girl. I wanted someday to say to her as well, "I'm sorry I ruined your life." Holding the phone in my hand right then, I had no doubt that it was the most exact sentence for the occasion.

That's all I could say. "I'm sorry." And pause. "I ruined your life." And then faster: "I'msorryIruinedyourlife." And slowly and clearly: "I'm sorry I ruined your life."

There was silence on the end of the line. I wasn't sure what it meant, if forgiveness was implied or being withheld, but it allowed me to say one more thing. "Good-bye."

...

"I'll do anything you tell me to," I said to you.

There was a new Bible on the table. You had borrowed it from a friend for some reason.

"Read to me from that while I do my yoga," you said.

I picked a random page. It was about an old man having sex with his daughters in a cave.

"Sex sounds so stale in the Bible," you said. "Why does it always just say that someone 'lay with' someone else? It sounds so boring."

I continued to read and I let my voice fall into a flat, lifeless monotone to see if you'd notice. You were twisted on the floor.

"Stop reading and come here," you said. "Lie with me now. Let's see what it feels like."

...

We saw an old lady on the bus talking to a teenage couple. The teens looked uncomfortable and moved away from her, into seats about ten feet away. The woman spoke louder. "Don't go there," she said. "Sex is sin and sin is death."

You put your left hand on my knee. I put my hands over your ears, so you wouldn't have to hear. Our protective instincts.

"People should just be nice," the lady said. When she got off the bus, we saw her still talking as she walked down the sidewalk.

. . .

We were at Victoria's Secret because I told you I would buy you something new and sexy. You asked me if I had any erotic underwear stories. I told you about Theresa, who wore bras that were too small for her, so that her breasts looked like they were constantly spilling out. I mentioned the first time I'd ever seen garter belts, during a one-night stand with an anorexic girl I used to work with. There was one girlfriend who didn't have a very good face but probably had the best ass I'd ever seen; she wore leopard-print panties. You made a face at me like you were offended, or maybe disgusted. I thought about backpedaling and saying that you had the best ass but I imagined you would sense the untruth of those words.

I walked around the store with you and tried not to imagine the other customers in their undergarments. There were a few other guys in there as well, but they mostly tried to blend into the wall while their wives or girlfriends or mistresses shopped around. A couple of them had the distinct look of men pensively exiting the doghouse. Their credit cards trembled between their twitchy fingers and thumbs.

I looked, perhaps perversely, at where the dressing rooms were, and I thought it was strangely erotic that some of the bras probably had had many women's nipples pressed into their cups. I was a little nervous about pointing out some of the bras I liked because there had been a time, early in our relationship, when I bought you a shirt and you got mad. You said I didn't know you well enough to shop for you. You said that men shouldn't clothes shop for women, but that women should clothes shop for men.

"I thought of another underwear story," I suddenly blurted out, before realizing it would probably be upsetting as well.

"What is it?" you asked.

"I think the most memorable underwear for me," I said carefully, "were these pair of silky panties that I took from my mom."

"Yeah," you said, as if it was no big deal. "And what about them?"

I tried to think of a funny way to say it. "I used them to whack off."

You laughed a little, just enough to let me know I was in the clear.

"And I sniffed her bras too," I said.

"That's nothing," you answered. "I used to smell my dad's underwear."

I wanted to ask you if you sniffed my underwear too, but part of me didn't really want to know.

...

I realized that I didn't know what formaldehyde was, but I didn't think you did either. We were at our neighborhood bar, getting drunk.

"Formaldehyde is something you put on walls to remove paint," you said.

"It's like really strong alcohol," I said. "Or you can put it in a dead person if you don't want them to disintegrate."

"You're thinking of those jars of dead babies," you told me.

I squinted at the bottles behind the bar to see if they had any formaldehyde. One bottle had a big radish or some kind of root in it that looked like a dead baby. My stomach roiled.

"I wonder what would happen if you soaked your hands in a tub of it," you said. "Would it keep them young?"

"I don't think it's good for . . . you . . . that way," I stammered. "What do you mean by *young*, anyway?"

"It would be kind of funny to have a withered hand," you said.

I drank more of my Mexican beer and imagined you with a withered hand. A beautiful, young withered hand.

. . .

Sometimes you had to take Ambien to fall asleep and it led to strange things. Like eating binges and loss of memory.

We woke up one morning and thought that someone had broken in and trashed the apartment. There were dirty dishes and half-eaten pieces of food everywhere, even in the hallway and around our bed. Cheetos were scattered all over the bathroom like shrapnel from a bomb. A jar of pickles was in the microwave and a frozen burrito was jammed into one of the toaster slots. In the other slot was a piece of ham.

"Did you hear anything at all last night?" I asked you.

"I went to bed right after you and slept like a rock," you told me.

The kids were up and watching television, seemingly unconcerned. "Did you and my mom try to do some kind of experimental cooking last night?" Maxine asked me.

"Is that burrito supposed to be in the toaster?" Vince asked.

You came out of the bedroom, rubbing your eyes and reading the label on the Ambien. I saw Cheeto dust on your fingers.

...

We went to your dad's farm for Christmas. He lived between Portland and Mount Hood, in a place called Sandy. Your sister and her husband and son were there too. Your dad gave Vince and Maxine a Wii. We opened presents and played virtual tennis all morning.

You and I had decided to take mushrooms in the afternoon, right before dinner and about an hour before we were going to meet some friends to go out for the evening. The kids were going to spend the night at your dad's.

I was eating turkey and mashed potatoes when I realized that the mushrooms had killed my taste buds already. I piled a bunch of food that I don't usually like on my plate—stuffing, squash, cranberry—and I ate it without the slightest grimace on my face. I asked for hot sauce and challenged your dad to a "hot-sauced turkey contest." He drank a beer and sweated through his new polo shirt. I was laughing and taking the smallest sips of water, chased with hot coffee. Suddenly, there were loud thrusts of wind banging against the window and snow swirling everywhere outside. Our friends called us and told us that they couldn't come and get us because they were already snowed in. You were looking out the window and holding the phone to your ear for several minutes, even though no one was on it to talk to anymore.

Your sister was standing behind you, wondering what you were doing. She said, "Hello?" and you started talking on the dead phone like she was on the line. I walked over to you and took the phone from your hand and turned you around to face your sister. You started laughing uncontrollably, at first like something was really funny and then like an insane person. Your laugh sounded backward: *Ah-ah-ah-ah-ah-ah-ah*. I was trying to usher you away, maybe to the guest bedroom in the back, but I felt the rush coming on too. My face stretched into a mad grin and my shoulders hunched. The house was surrounded by a tornado of snow and I realized that we were stuck inside with everyone while our brains turned to goo in our heads. Your dad was shaking his head like he knew what was going on, but your sister asked in the most innocent way, "What could be so funny?"

Once we were alone, we quietly tried to come up with a game plan. We knew we couldn't stay inside with the sober family so we told your dad that we'd go check on the cows. We found them in the two shelters by the pasture, but there was one that was still out in the storm, walking in circles, almost like she was enjoying it. We stumbled around in the wind and tried to steer the animal to a shelter, but it turned at the last moment and headed back toward the middle of the pasture. "She likes it!" you shouted through the wind. You climbed up and got on her back. "Come on," you said. I tried to climb on too, but just draped myself over her like a blanket. I felt warm like a blanket. You ran your fingers through my hair and I stared down and watched the cow's hooves dancing around the glowing white dance floor.

. . .

I took Maxine to Dairy Queen for dessert one night when Vince was at his mom's and you were working late. I got a Hot Fudge Volcano or something like that. Maxine got a dipped cone. She carefully ate the strawberry-colored shell from the ice cream swirl as she studied a flier that listed the calories for everything on the menu. "Yours is like five thousand calories," she said, looking gravely at me. "Mine is only 340."

I tried to snatch the flier but she held it away from me. "Maybe you should save some for my mom," she said.

"I can handle it," I said. I took another lumpy bite of brownie smeared with whipped cream and hot fudge, but her words had a sly effect on me. I was already starting to feel full.

I didn't get many chances to talk to Maxine one on one, so when I did it took me a while to get the conversation going into a comfortable flow.

"How's junior high life?" I asked.

"It's fine," she said. Her usual response to any topic she didn't want to speak further on.

"How is band going?"

"It's fine too."

"Do you ever see Vince in the hallways or at lunch?"

"The eighth graders and seventh graders have different lunch times. But yeah, I see him sometimes, by his locker. My friend Phoebe thinks he's cute, but I haven't told him."

I felt a flash of pride that a girl found Vince attractive. I wanted to ask about this Phoebe but I also wanted to stay on topic.

"Does he hang out with many kids?" I asked.

"Do you want to hire me as a spy or something?" she asked.

I chewed up some more brownie and spooned melted ice cream into my mouth. I wondered if she was serious about her offer. Talking to Vince was more difficult than conversing with Maxine, and I was curious about his social life at school.

Maxine's face took on a more serious squint. "Is that why you brought me here? You thought, *I'll give her some ice cream and she'll tell me what's wrong with Vince?* Is that the scoop you're looking for?"

It felt like we were suddenly starring in some sort of film noir. I couldn't figure out my next line. I looked down at my clichéd raincoat and black leather shoes. My right hand dropped the plastic spoon into the mess of dairy below it and then shot up to my lips. I hadn't smoked in years but my fingers shook like I was holding a cigarette there. I craved a cup of coffee as black as the sky outside. This twelve-year-old girl in front of me seemed like someone new, someone I didn't know. Her gaze was steady on mine and I waited for more words, sharp and fast, to come out of her mouth. But she waited for me, her cards on the table. Ice cream dripping down her fingers.

...

We were driving around and they were playing eighties music on the radio. They were playing "Sexy & 17."

"There was a time when I really liked the Stray Cats. I had their first two albums," I said to you.

"I don't really remember them," you said. "But my brother may have liked them. He had a lot of cassettes."

A song by Supertramp came on. It was "Take the Long Way Home."

"This song reminds me more of the seventies than the eighties," I said. "I always thought it was weird that they say 'wife' in this song. I mean, rock bands don't talk about marriage much."

You patted me on the knee and said, "Maybe that's why it sounds so sad." We laughed a little but I realized you were right. The song talks about the wife treating the guy like a piece of furniture and then the wife says the guy is losing his sanity.

No wonder he takes the long way home.

I pictured the *Breakfast in America* cover in my mind: the waitress with the platter held above her head, the glass of orange juice on the platter, the New York skyscrapers in the background. The Twin Towers. I remembered a lot about it, even though I only ever listened to my cousin's copy. On eight-track tape.

I almost started crying for some reason. I wondered if Vince would have memories of music like this when he got older. Notes and rhythms and lyrics that worked like scents. You looked over at me and saw that my mood had changed.

A song by Elton John came on. "I Guess That's Why They Call It the Blues." You slouched forward in the passenger seat and put your hands up to your face. I couldn't tell if you were laughing or crying. "I hope Maxine has songs that make her feel things," you said. I put my hand out for you, and you grabbed it. Your palms were wet. "God damn you, Elton John," you said.

...

You told me about some scientific study that said people find their sexual partners more attractive than they actually are. I reevaluated some of my past girlfriends and realized that the study is probably right.

We looked straight at each other for a long time, as if we were now other people, recalibrating each other's level of attractiveness. All this did was make me think of one of our first nights together. We were in my car in a giant parking lot by the shopping mall. The windshield wipers on my car weren't working, so we sat there and waited for the rain to ease up. But it just got stormier, and the rain got heavier and pounded on top of the car like someone playing a drum solo. Sometimes other cars would drive by and their headlights would scan over your smiling face. The rain was pouring down the car windows like we were under a waterfall, and these lights reflected that water over your face like it was melting and melting and melting, but your smile got bigger, like your face was saying, *I'm so glad we're trapped here!* That was the moment I knew we'd probably be together forever. If we both lived to be ninety and died and went to heaven or someplace like heaven, we'd meet there and fall in love all over again. We sat in that car, with the rain and passing lights and the willingness to wait forever to start moving again. Our molecules seemed to fuse together right there. Our cells. Our DNA.

I believed in science. I believed in your smile.

. . .

When Vince was younger, he used to talk nonstop. He would start telling a story about something, and then it would spin off into some fantastical territory. He would dominate conversations so much that I would sometimes have to tell him to wrap it up. But I didn't want to sound mean, so I would just say something like, "That sure is some story, Vince. Tell us how it ends."

Some of those first times when all four of us would be driving somewhere together, Vince would get started on a new story, and the rest of us would be surrounded by his breathless words for thirty minutes. You and I would zone out on the lines in the road, the country scenery and clouds in the sky. Maxine would seem interested at first and then she would curl into a ball like she was angry.

When Vince turned into a teenager, it was like he'd taken some secret oath to withhold information from parental figures. Our conversations became mostly limited to my questions and his one-word responses.

"How was school today?"

"Good."

"Do you have any homework?"

"Some."

"Did you have lunch with Roberto today?"

"Yeah."

"Wanna go shoot some baskets?"

"No."

One day I went in his room to put some clothes away. He was working on his computer, writing a paper for a class. It was dark in his room, so I turned on his light. "Don't turn on the light. I don't want the light on," he said sharply. I was agitated by his tone and let it show. "Just settle down. I'm trying to do you a favor," I said. "But I was on a good roll," he said. I didn't have a calm response ready, like a good father should. I blurted out, "You don't have to be so dickish about it." I flicked his light back off when I left. The rest of the night we were cold to each other.

The next morning was Sunday. We had omelets for break-fast, and then Vince went to his room and started playing a video game. I went in and sat down next to him. I asked him to set down his controller and tried to gather some authorita-tive composure. "I don't like it when you talk to me like you did last night," I said. "It makes me feel bad."

"Okay," he said.

"I'm glad you're serious about your homework, but you could have been nicer in that situation."

"I'm sorry," he said.

"All right," I said. And then I suddenly laughed for some reason. Maybe it was because I felt a kind of small victory had occurred, a tiny and jagged lesson learned (the sensation like a pebble extracted from a shoe). Maybe it was because I realized that his response to my interruption—*Turn off the light! Leave me alone!*—was one I wished I could give to someone.

I slid my arm around him and gave him a hug, though he did not return the squeeze. I heard a character's voice from his video game interrupt our moment. "Sergeant! Sergeant! We have to get this mission started, Sergeant! What are you doing?"

# YEAR FIVE

You seemed troubled all day long, and then at night you told me that you had been wondering if dead people could watch us from heaven or wherever they were at. These were the things we talked about on quiet nights.

"Can my old neighbor, Mark, who died in a car crash, see everything I'm doing, or is it just my mom and the people I love who can see me?"

"That's a good question," I said. "But I think, if they're in heaven, they can only see us if we're outside or in a wide-open space."

"Maybe heaven is just being able to watch people. Like voyeurism," you said. "And maybe in hell you can't see people at all, and that's what makes it so painful."

We had the obituary section of the newspaper spread out on the coffee table in front of us.

"I sometimes wonder if my grandfather can watch me," I said. "Mostly when I'm masturbating or going to the bathroom. I wonder if only certain dead people can see my bowel movements."

"Imagine heaven with a bunch of toilet cams!"

We thought about that while looking at the photographs of all the people who had died in the last few days. The obituaries were six pages long.

You took my hand and said we needed to go somewhere. We walked a few blocks to where a middle school was. It was a warm night. We walked through the grassy playground and found a discarded Frisbee that we tossed back and forth. It was the kind with a big hole in the middle, like a flying glow-in-the-dark halo. Then you ran toward me and flopped on the ground. You shimmied out of your pants and told me to join you. We held each other tight and made love in the dark. Some grass was flattened, torn out, destroyed. The big clear sky above us made us feel protected, like we'd never die. We hoped that God and the rest of heaven was watching us. We showed them what we were like on earth.

...

Our love was hardly ever equal. The intensity of our admiration was proportional to the amount of housework we did. There were months when one of us did everything for the other and then we switched places. It was always easy to figure out who was more in love: who was cooking dinner, cleaning the bathroom, sorting the laundry, and keeping track of all the activities on the calendar. I can't really remember what the other person was doing while all these responsibilities were getting done, but that person eventually worked up enough guilty energy to do some work too.

But the more this shifting happened, the more wobbly we felt. I worried that you were getting bored with me, that you were outgrowing me.

One night in bed, when I wasn't sure if you were listening or even awake, I said, "You're going to pass me by. You've already slid by. You're beyond me. On some other side. Some side I can't even see."

I listened to your breathing in the dark. It did not change.

...

You told me about seeing an old friend at the store and how she asked you if we were still a couple. You said she gave you a disappointed look when you told her that we were still together. You did tell her, though, that we had broken up a few times and we were now seeing a therapist. She smiled warmly, maybe condescendingly, when you told her that part. She put her hand on your arm, even stroked your wrist a little. This was a friend whose opinion you used to respect, someone who has been married to her high school sweetheart for almost twenty years, even though she got more miserable every year.

"What has he done to prove himself to you?" she asked you.

You remembered how I bought you flowers, how I said I was sorry, how I undressed you like a starving man, but that was about it. You told your friend that it had to do with having time apart and how that put things in perspective. But in the back of your mind, several sad, defeated thoughts scrolled by: *This is as good as it will ever get now . . . I can't remember what I was unhappy about . . . I have always overreacted about simple things . . . Why should someone prove himself to me when I can't even prove myself to anyone? . . . It's nice to have someone help with the bills and rent . . . I don't want to die alone.*

Your friend gave you a hug and whispered something that sounded like a daily affirmation into your ear before she said good-bye. You continued shopping, even though you were quietly filling with an uneasy mix of shame and anger. When you got to the checkout stand, you saw your friend thumbing slowly through some garish gossip magazine with headlines about affairs, cellulite, and movie stars in rehab. Her eyes sparkled and her mouth twitched lightly with drool. She looked like she wanted to dive into the magazine and fix everyone's shitty world.

. . .

We found someone to give Vince guitar lessons and he picked it up quickly. In just a few months, they were playing songs from Jim Croce, the Beatles, Nirvana, and some cheesy European metal bands that Vince liked. I would sit in the back bedroom and listen in while I read a library book or put laundry away. The whole apartment would be quiet and it was so peaceful to listen to Vince playing alongside his jazz-trained teacher—sometimes struggling to find the right finger position while keeping the tempo. Sometimes he'd keep pace with his teacher impressively.

During these forty-five minutes each week, I'd often recall my own guitar lessons. I was in junior high and I would take lessons from my history teacher, Mr. Drucker, after school. When we first started, he taught me to play "Smoke on the Water" and then asked me what song I wanted to learn as a goal. I chose "The Joker" by Steve Miller. About two months later, I had learned the song, but I couldn't sing and play at the same time. Mr. Drucker sang the words. When he got to the line, "Some people call me Maurice," I would make the whistling sound and try not to laugh.

Mr. Drucker died later that year when he was riding his bike home at night and was hit by a drunk driver. I didn't pick up a guitar again for a long time.

...

Vince was playing some of his new favorite CDs for me in the car as I drove him to the dentist. The songs sounded like pop music from when I was a teenager, but filtered through a couple of decades of trying too hard.

But they also sounded like the kind of songs I might have liked if they had been around when I was his age. I felt torn about how to react. I was mildly embarrassed for him, and as a result, I also felt embarrassment for my past self. Had my parents felt the same way about the music I listened to? And had their parents felt the same way? And their parents before that?

I wondered if there had been a whole generation of parents long ago who were agitated by the emerging popularity of the harmonica. I made a mental note to look up the history of the harmonica when I got home.

Vince said, "Listen to this part." A loud guitar part started to slow down and a skitter of drums twisted the song into a new tempo, a new mood. Again, it reminded me of something I'd loved in the past. One of my favorite bands, but this time with more eyeliner, more money. I tried to act impressed and I said, "That was cool." The song went on. I was feeling my age, and I said in my head, *That was cool . . . That. Was. Cool.*

. . .

You took me to a strip club and we noticed that all the dancers had tattoos. We looked around and saw that all the customers had tattoos as well. "I guess it's kind of unusual that we don't have tattoos," you said.

I put my hand around my mouth and whispered back to you, "I think we should get tattoos that say, *I don't have a tattoo.*"

"Or maybe a tattoo that says, *Not a real tattoo,*" you said.

We finished up our fourth drinks and talked to the dancer whose legs had tattooed lines going up the backs of them, like she was wearing some sexy vintage panty hose. She also had an elaborately inked peacock going up her left arm and shoulder. Her knuckles said K-A-Y-A, even though she told us her name was Hurricane.

"What's your names?" she asked us.

We made up names for some reason. Shawn and Shawna.

When we went back to the bar, we talked about how the tattoos were too much like a shield, or a substitute for clothes.

"These girls are not one hundred percent naked," I decided. "They have tattoos." We came up with all kinds of theories and then you looked up "strippers without tattoos" on your iPhone and there were no matches.

"I guess we're stuck here," you said. We borrowed Sharpies from the bartender and asked each of the dancers to mark us. "We don't want to be naked either," you told the tall redhead with stars on her ass.

. . .

I went to bed a few minutes before you one night and decided to lie the opposite direction in bed, so my head was where my feet usually were. My feet were sticking out and resting on the pillow, like a weird joke. I heard you getting out of the bath and then brushing your teeth. I readied myself anxiously but quietly in this new position. This probably wasn't quite what you had in mind when you said you wanted to try some new things in the bedroom. You crawled into bed and hugged my legs against your chest. At first you froze, but then you started kissing my ticklish ankles. Your toes brushed my cheeks. The night seemed upside down.

. . .

You were in the hospital and I was at work, even though I didn't want to be there. It was the day after you had back surgery and you were high on some kind of painkiller. You kept calling me on my cell phone while I was at work, and I was both concerned and annoyed. But I took a break and snuck into an empty room to listen to you when you started talking about the feeling between your legs. Room 529, where we had spent time together in the past—our favorite room.

"It feels like a bunch of small birds," you said.

I wasn't sure if that was an erotic feeling. "What are the birds doing?" I asked.

"They're flying, but in slow motion," you said. "Their wings are so soft. I have a parachute but nothing else on. I'm falling and I feel the wind and wings, and I thought about you."

I asked you what I was doing in your thoughts.

"You're waiting for me on the ground, on your back. Your hands are up, ready to catch me."

You asked if I was excited and I said yes. I heard your bedsheets rustle. I imagined you melting into them.

"I want you to touch yourself," you said. "Tell me what you do when you catch me."

I told you that I wanted you to land like that, legs spread, on top of my face, against my lips. The parachute would cover us softly. You made a long moaning sound when I said that and then you said, *Uh-huh* over and over until it turned into heavy breathing.

"Your face is the best place to land," you said. "I want to make a nest in your mouth."

...

For a while, you became more aggressive with your biting and your need for me to bite you. I remember when we first met you didn't like it at all. I'd often bite your lips a little when we kissed and you'd always yelp and tell me to stop. I think one time you said, "I'm not a dog!"

Then, in our fifth year, when we were having sex, you'd sometimes arch your neck and pull my face into it. I couldn't figure out if this was because you were fantasizing about some kind of sexy movie vampire or if you were really into the feeling of it. I didn't close my jaw, I just pressed my teeth against your skin.

When you bit me, you closed your jaw. One time, it was such a hard pinch on my neck that my hands flew up and pushed you away. I swore and turned over. It felt like you did it on purpose and I was trying not to get mad.

You touched me on the back softly and whispered, "Are you still hard?"

...

In the morning, we were making breakfast and coffee as we waited for your brother to wake up. He was staying with us for a few days, visiting us from Denver, where he had just moved. You were wearing new jeans and a white T-shirt. I liked it when you wore a black bra under a white shirt. There is something assertive but coquettish about that look, like a woman undressing in her tenth-floor hotel room with the curtains open.

I rubbed the rim of my empty coffee cup on your ass cheek. "Let me get some of this ass in my coffee," I said with a perverted sneer. I was like a bartender salting a margarita glass. You were bent over, putting biscuits in the oven, moving your hips in circles like a tease.

"Do you want honey in your biscuits?" you asked.

"I like your pants," I said.

When your brother came out ten minutes later, he asked if we had anything he could put in his coffee.

"You want cream?" I asked him.

"You got honey?" he asked. He was smiling and rubbing the sleep from his eyes. I felt his focus scanning between you and me. You were making eggs next to me as I poured the cream. "I like your pants," he said to one of us.

We said "thanks" at the same time. Then a few moments of silence.

...

We were out at a local club where a new band was playing. The bass player of the band was a famous young actor, so there were a lot of young women dressed their sexiest. Most of them stood near his side of the stage. People were jumping up and down all around us. The drum sounds bounced against the chugging guitars. "I'm being felt up by like twenty people," you shouted in my ear, but you were smiling as we swayed with the crowd.

I felt badly for the lead singer. No one was looking at him. They all watched the famous bass player, who did nothing exciting and even had his back to the audience.

I remember the first show we went to, at a small club where my friend's band was headlining. It was a mellow show and we sat at a table near the stage, holding hands. We did not have to guard our drinks from people bumping into us. We could see and hear everything, and my friend even dedicated a song to us.

I loved that show but I loved this show too, in a different way. That one was intimate and this one was chaotic. When the bass player finally turned around, the crowd went crazy. The beautiful young women around me had the shyest white-blonde hairs on their arms. I could almost feel their softness as they all rose above me, swaying like flowers. You were pushed into me and I caught you. Your laugh smelled like good whiskey. We couldn't see the stage anymore but we watched through all the camera phones in the air. The bass player was smiling, the bass player was smiling, and the bass player was smiling.

. . .

One night we went out to dinner with your father and he kept asking us if we were going to get married soon. He didn't like it when we danced around topics of conversation so we tried to explain it clearly to him. "We've both been married before," you said. "And it wasn't that fun the first time."

Your father sipped on his decaf coffee and shook his head slowly with a frown.

"You were lucky to have just one wife," I said, realizing I was going into possibly unwelcome territory. "A good wife," I added. "Now imagine getting married again. It would feel less exciting or something."

I had to be careful not to say anything that would make you feel unappreciated. It was especially hard not to think about Cynthia, especially since we had gone to her funeral a month earlier. Maybe what I'd said about "getting married again" was wrong. Maybe your father would have married Cynthia in a hot second.

I was sitting between you and your father and I felt like I was suddenly juggling some delicate plates. No one spoke and I felt the silence mangling the message I was trying to get across. Was I really the best spokesman in this situation? I felt the ghost of Cynthia and the ghost of your mom also silently judging me from somewhere else in the room. I could almost hear plates shattering on the ground.

You raised your finger and jumped in before I could make another utterance. "Marriage is harder to navigate these days. It's almost too comfortable." You took a long drink of water, like you were stalling for time. "We like to grow and be challenged. When people are legally bound it creates a psychological obstacle."

"Who's *we*? What *people*?" your father asked. He cocked his head. He cocked his bushy eyebrow.

"It's not the fifties anymore," you said.

"Fifties?" your father almost shouted.

"Sixties, seventies. Whatever," you said.

The conversation had officially puttered into a dead end. We ate our dinner, trying to be polite the rest of the night. There was no dessert. A small squabble over the bill provided some excitement but your father eventually wrestled it away from us. I held the door open for the two of you, holding hands. I trailed a little behind and watched your matching

strides. You were the same height as your father. You looked
up at something in the sky, and he looked there too.

...

Sometimes the kids were both a little moody at the same time.
But thankfully that wasn't usually the case. If one of them
was off, then the other one was friendlier to us. It's like they
were always playing a game of good cop/bad cop. One night,
Maxine stayed in her room with her lights off and sad music playing too loudly. Vince helped us with the after-dinner
cleanup and even watched TV with us. A show we didn't think
he liked. He asked if I could show him how to shave for real.
We had only pretended before.

I remembered learning to shave, but for a long time I used an
electric razor. I was scared of real razors until I was almost thirty.

I told Vince that he had to be very careful, and then we
lathered up. He had only the faintest wisp of fuzz around his
lips and chin. We watched each other in the mirror, and when
I dragged the razor down my cheek, Vince grimaced a little at
the soft scraping sound.

When he brought the razor up to his face, I stood behind
him and grabbed his arm and tried to help him angle it, like a
tennis teacher trying to show a student how to swing a racket.
"Push it against your skin, not into it," I told him. His eyes lit
up as he did it and his scrape was just slightly quieter than mine.

When we were done, I asked him what was wrong with
Maxine and he shrugged, almost like he was too cool to care.
"I don't know," he said. "Girl stuff, I bet."

. . .

You got me a blank notebook one year for Christmas and I wanted to fill it with pictures and writing for you. But I had a hard time doing that for some reason, so I found an old cassette player and recorded some thoughts for you instead. I pretended like it was an oral diary, and every few days I would talk about things we'd done. Then I would record the sounds of our neighborhood—the announcements from the train stops, the birds taunting the cat in the yard, our kids riding their noisy skateboards and bikes. I would talk about holding your hand at the movies. I recorded the sound of our mailbox opening. One night, when you came home late, I captured the sound of the car crackling up the driveway and me whispering, "Welcome home. Now you're home."

Eventually, I cut a shallow space out of the meat of the notebook and put the finished cassette in there. I had Vince and Maxine decorate the outside of the notebook. Then I gave it to you on the morning of the next Christmas. We listened to it later that day, while the kids were in their rooms. They heard some of the tape, but there were parts that were meant only for you. We listened to all of it a few more times that week, and then, on New Year's Day, we wrapped it in an old shirt of mine and buried it in the backyard.

. . .

We read in bed and I would hold my book firmly, sometimes reading forty or fifty pages before I was tired.

You would lie beside me, also trying to read, but I saw, out of the corner of my eye, your book drooping out of your hands and then your body jolting awake. You lost your place often and your eyes couldn't stay open.

Sometimes I wanted to catch your book for you, so you wouldn't lose your place. I was also afraid that you might, one night, break your nose and blacken your eye with a heavy book, slipped from your own fingers. That made it harder for me to concentrate on my own book.

I said, "Just put the book down and roll over before you hurt yourself." You waved your hand at me like a mad old lady and said, "I'm awake, all right? I'm awake."

Our cat sighed from the corner of the room. When I turned a page in my book, it sounded like a shovel picking up sand. There was a soft ticking that came from outside our window. Maybe a tree branch. Maybe the moonlight.

...

You were cleaning the apartment one day while I tried to relax on the couch. You vacuumed and dusted near me, bustling around and making a big show of your work. You noticed a mark on the back of the couch—a dark skid on the soft cream fabric. "What is that?" you said. I looked and said I didn't know. "We've had this couch for less than a year," you said, like it was some twisted form of accusation.

The mark was in a place that people probably wouldn't see. You said that didn't matter. "Whenever I look at the couch now, my eyes will always go to that mark."

I knew that was the unfortunate truth of the matter. When something clean and perfect got tarnished, it was the main thing you saw after that. It was the beginning of something getting old.

...

Maxine said she had something to tell me, so we walked to the park down the street. "We need to talk," she said. For some reason, even coming from a fourteen-year-old, those words sounded ominous and terrifying. She was bouncing a basketball, dodging the sidewalk cracks. It helped to alleviate some tension.

"It's about Vince," she said. "I've been watching him."

"And how is he?" I asked.

She stopped bouncing the ball and handed it to me. She took out her cell phone. "He doesn't eat lunch with Roberto," she said. She showed me a blurry photo on her phone: Vince sitting by himself, eating lunch on a bench outside the school library.

"Does he eat lunch with anyone?" I asked.

"I don't think so," Maxine said. "Not just that, though. I don't think there *is* a Roberto."

...

I remember when Vince started going to movies in theaters with me, but the previews for other movies frightened him. Maybe they were too loud, or just too unfamiliar to him, so we would wait outside the door until they ended.

You told me about a time when Maxine was scared of your grandfather's teeth, the way he left them out in a glass of denture cleaner in the bathroom. Maxine couldn't go to the bathroom in the morning until your grandfather put his teeth back in.

I told you about how I was scared of grasshoppers when I was a kid. All the neighborhood kids would catch them, but I ran away from them and hated the sound they made, like broken sprinklers.

You told me that you had criktaphobia, a word I'm sure you made up. It was a condition that involved a fear of ticking clocks. When you heard one in a quiet room, you'd have to make a louder sound to cover it—a clucking or a humming. You got dizzy doing this, the air tightening up around you until you felt yourself spin away.

I thought these were the kinds of fears that love could cure. I waited to see.

...

Sometimes I have vague memories of going down twisty slides with Vince in my lap. Getting snow cones at the public pool. Playing "horsie" with him. Reading to him at bedtime. I wish you could have seen me back then.

...

Vince and I used to go to this really cool retro arcade and play video games every few months. I realized that we hadn't gone in about two years and asked him if he wanted to go with me on a Saturday. We used to play this funny two-player game where we competed against each other, guiding our characters through an obstacle course where we'd dodge fireballs, lightning, and other damaging things. At the end of the game, the loser would fall through a hole into a dungeon and get eaten by a giant creature. I usually let Vince win, so he wouldn't have to see the creature spit out his skull.

When I asked him if he wanted to go, though, he hesitantly said that he couldn't. "I'm meeting Roberto for lunch," he said.

I thought it was strange that he would say they were meeting for lunch. It sounded so grown-up, so not fun. At least not as fun as going to the park or the mall or the arcade.

"Want me to give you a ride somewhere?" I asked.

"No."

"Need some money?"

"No."

"Okay," I said. "Well, I guess I'll see you later then."

I felt left out. I started to wonder if I'd ever go to that arcade again.

After Vince left, I went for a drive by myself. I cruised slowly by the arcade and thought of stopping. But I pictured myself going in there, by myself, and it made me feel nervous for some reason. I circled around again and started to feel sick. I pulled over and shut off the car. I got out and started walking toward the door, then changed my mind. Back in the driver's seat of the car, I was indecisive and confused. I felt like I was missing something. I felt useless.

. . .

"Should we try to have our own?" you asked me. We were at the neighborhood park, watching other people with their young children. *It might be what we need,* I thought. It would give us a shared experience, our own child that nobody else could interfere with.

"It seems like if it were going to happen, it would have by now," I said. We hadn't really been careful with our birth control for at least a year. I could feel you thinking about that and didn't want you to misunderstand what I meant. "Maybe I can't do it," I said. "Maybe I don't have good swimmers."

You looked at me and squeezed my arm. "It's probably me," you said. "I put too much shit in my body."

"We don't really want to be those old parents at the elementary school anyway," I said. "Everyone thinking that we're the grandparents, or worse—not cool."

I got you to laugh at that, but for a moment I thought you were crying. "Look at these kids though," you said. "We could do so much better."

. . .

When I left my wife, Sheryl, she was sad for only a couple of days before she was ready to move on. She called me and asked if it would bother me if she slept with a sixty-eight-year-old man. A man down the hall from her named Pablo.

"That's as old as your grandfather," I said.

"But I have feelings for him," she told me.

"Why don't you take it slow?" I said. "Maybe form a relationship first."

"I kind of just want to see what it would be like," she said. "He said he hasn't had sex in fifteen years."

There were a few seconds of silence while I tried to think of a way to get off the phone.

"Are you jealous?" she asked.

For some reason, I became emotional and started weeping. I wasn't jealous, but something else about the conversation jabbed me uncomfortably. I put myself in Pablo's worn-out shoes, facing those last gray years with saggy flesh, cracked bifocals, and garlicky breath.

My estranged wife would be like an angel, her young, smooth hand inside his old, hairy hand, walking him into the fluorescent light of some sacred kind of kingdom.

. . .

I decided to take Vince somewhere with a lot of kids. I thought maybe it would be the easiest place to forget about a serious talk. But first we had to have the serious talk.

We sat in the car, in the parking lot, the sounds of the carnival rides drifting over to us. The amusement park was right in front of us, waiting. We could see the roller coaster and the Tilt-a-Whirl shining in the sun.

I knew it was probably best just to start talking instead of easing into it or prefacing it. It would be better if I didn't give Vince time to put a wall between us.

"Who's this Roberto character?" I asked him.

I could see him tense up. "What do you mean?" he said.

"I asked your school counselor and she said there wasn't anyone in your school with that name," I said. I tried not to sound like I was accusing him of anything.

"I have to go to the bathroom," he said.

"We'll go inside in a minute. You're not in trouble, but I just want to figure this out. It's no big deal," I said.

"I have to go," Vince said a little louder.

"Don't yell," I said. "We'll go in a second. Did you make him up?"

"I don't know," said Vince. "I'm not sure why."

"You have friends, though," I said. "You don't have to make up any."

"But I don't like my friends most of the time," he answered. There was a little pout in his voice. He started telling me about how some of his friends had girlfriends now, how some of his friends were going to a new school next year, how some of his friends said they didn't like him as much as they used to. He said his friends were turning into other things: jocks, stoners, popular kids who belonged to every school club, emo kids with angry divorced parents. I wondered if Vince would ever consider himself a product of "angry divorced parents."

He wanted to have a friend he could control, so he invented Roberto. I asked him if it was more for our sake or for his own.

"Both," he said, and then started crying. Maybe it was because of me, I thought. Or because of the way my life's confusion made us feel unsettled. He just wanted something in his life that *he* could control.

"We can work on it together," I said, trying to be reassuring.

"How are we going to do that?" he said with a little frustration in his voice.

"I know it's hard right now," I told him. "But it gets easier soon. You'll have this friend stuff figured out in the next couple of years." I realized that a "couple of years" probably sounded like forever to a fifteen-year-old.

When we got out of the car, I felt like things were more open between us. I put my hand on his shoulder and he let it stay there for a few moments. When we entered the park, a swirl of kids and teens around us, he subtly shrugged me off.

An hour later, we were in the bumper cars, crashing into each other a few times before deciding to gang up on the other kids.

...

Vince and I were out for a hike around Forest Park. We liked walking on this specific trail during the summer because all the trees made it feel cooler than it was. When we first started coming out here, it would take a long time to complete the route because Vince would walk so slow and want to gather every big stick and read every sign. I would have a dozen sticks under my arms by the time we got back to the car. Then I'd have to put the sticks in the trunk, and we'd take them home and add them to the bucket by the back door. Sometimes we would find a rock that looked like an arrowhead and we'd tie it to the end of a stick and pretend it was a spear. We had an old bow from an archery set and we would launch these homemade arrows, wobbly, across the yard. His mom would watch us and smile. We weren't a broken family just yet.

But Vince got older and didn't collect sticks anymore. We walked in silence then, rarely stopping. I couldn't think of anything to say. I'd ask a question and the answer would be short and final. Not like he was mad, but like he wanted to be independent. Maybe solitary. Still, we kept going out on the trails because I hoped the time added up to something. I kind of wished he would still jump on my back for a piggyback ride, but he was too big for that. The only time I'd get to pick him up then was when we fake wrestled. So I fake wrestled with him sometimes, full of exaggerated aggression. I picked him up like I was going to body slam him, but I was just doing it to press him against me, to feel his weight again.

...

I couldn't imagine Vince's first kiss. But for some reason, I could see Maxine kissing someone. Not that I liked to imagine that. But she's your daughter and she seemed to exhibit an early grace, a mature demeanor. Vince was merely a teenage boy who would wear too much cologne if he wasn't monitored. Plus, he still needed to be reminded to cut his toenails. At least he had less acne than I did at that age. That was one small victory in his adolescence.

I remember my first kiss. It feels so long ago. I didn't want to open my mouth because the girl had braces. I had braces too. We were both fifteen. I wanted to suck all the lipstick off

Jennifer Malloy's lips. I thought the lipstick was what tasted so good.

Vince had a mannequin head in his room for a while. Something he'd needed to get for a school project. One time I saw it sticking out of his backpack, the hard, smooth forehead and reddish-blonde hairdresser hair. It actually looked a little like Jennifer Malloy. I wondered if he practiced on it.

...

Whenever you and I were alone in an elevator, we would crash together and make out, like it was some kind of ritual or elevator tradition. It was something wired in us.

Maybe it stemmed from one of our first dates, when we had nowhere to be alone, and so we found the tallest building downtown and rode the elevator up and down for several minutes. Whenever the door started to open, we would separate and pretend to talk about a business meeting we had just gotten out of. Then when the people got off on their floor, we would start kissing and fondling again. It was like a game. Red light. Green light.

...

It was the first warm day of the year, but you said you'd never wear shorts again. Your legs were shot, you told me.

"Skirts are okay," you said. "But nothing that will show my knees."

"I don't think I've even bought shorts for five years. What kind of shorts do people wear anymore?" I asked.

"You can't wear saggy, baggy shorts. Only kids wear those. And you can't wear hemmed jean shorts or Hawaiian shorts. Only old folks wear those," you explained.

"Like they issue those shorts to you when you check into the nursing home," I said.

"Your legs are cute," you said sweetly.

"No one wants to see forty-year-old legs. Maybe I'll just be one of those guys who wear jeans all the time, like James Dean did. Do you think he had several pairs of the same Levi's? Did James Dean ever wear shorts?"

"You're not forty," you said.

"Close enough," I said.

We were taking the kids to the park to play basketball, so I kept looking for something besides pants. I found one pair of shorts with the top button missing, another pair that was too small, and a pair that I'd worn several years ago and felt self-conscious in and never wore again. I found a pair of old plaid pants that I'd bought for a costume party and I pulled them out. You grabbed the scissors and cut off the legs, just above the knees. "Not too high," I said. I felt the steel of one of the scissor blades moving through my leg hair.

"We're ready!" we heard Maxine yell from the other room.

You stood back and admired your handiwork.

"If I'm wearing these, you have to wear shorts too," I said. It felt like a dare. You rummaged through the back of your closet and pulled out a ratty pair of jeans. They had holes in the knees and you tore them more and snipped them apart there.

"I can see your knees," I said when you slid them on.

"If the kids say anything, I'm coming right back and putting on a long skirt," you said.

We went to the park and played two on two and P-I-G, and the warm air and bright sun made us feel like we'd been set free after being trapped inside all winter and spring. My legs felt new and light.

"We're both wearing shorts!" I whispered excitedly to you. "How does it feel?"

"Shut up," you said.

I made a half-court shot that would have given you and the kids P-I-G, but you made the shot too, and then Maxine and then Vince. It felt like some kind of family accomplishment or miracle, like we should have been awarded a trophy, or at least a certificate from whatever god was watching us.

. . .

There is nothing I can do about these varicose veins. There is nothing you can do about your slightly crooked teeth. There is nothing I can do about my eyebrows. There is nothing you can do about that sick feeling you get when you're going to get a pedicure. These are things that will last forever. We must learn to love them. Somehow, some way.

. . .

"Did anything ever happen with you and Daniel?" you asked me one night after we watched a movie. We were on the couch, sharing a pint of ice cream and drinking whiskey.

The movie we'd just seen had a gay character who seduces a straight man.

"He's not really my type," I said, in a way that was meant to sound casual.

"What would be your type?" you asked me.

I could tell you were getting serious and I tried to diffuse the moment. "I'm just kidding, baby. What would make you think about that?"

"Sometimes you guys would act funny around me. Especially after you drank a little. I don't like to mix him with my boyfriends, you know?"

I was so glad your brother had moved away then. I was so glad that I'd pushed him away that last weekend he'd lived in Portland, when he'd come on to me not once, not twice, but three times. I was so glad that he was in Denver and that you didn't like Denver.

...

I was still having a hard time speaking with Vince when I was alone with him. He was becoming a moody teenager and didn't speak much. We sometimes took the MAX train at the same time in the morning. Him to school and me to work. Usually we'd stand apart from each other because there were other kids from his school around and he was trying to act cool around them. I wondered if he would be embarrassed if I tried to talk to him. He would get off the train a couple of stops before me and I'd give him a subtle nod from across the aisle, as if to say, "Have a good day."

One day, I separated myself a little farther from him and got on a totally different part of the train. When it came to his stop, I couldn't see him getting off. I couldn't give him the nod. I felt guilty the rest of the day.

A few days later, we were alone in our car. I picked him up from the mall after I'd attended a parent-teacher conference at his school. He was getting good grades and all his teachers liked him. I wanted to tell him that I loved him. It seemed like I hadn't said it in a while. But we drove in silence and I couldn't speak. I told myself I better say it. I thought if I didn't utter those words, they would become harder to say as he got older, quieter, maybe less needing of me.

I felt myself getting choked up, so I just put my hand on his knee and said, "I'm proud of you."

...

"I can't find any music videos by Beethoven," Maxine said, looking around YouTube on her computer. For some reason, she was on the brink of tears.

"They didn't make videos for music like that. It was too long ago," I said, with a small attempt at a laugh.

"Don't laugh at me," she said. She made two sniffling sounds and then I saw a tear drop from her eye.

"There are movies about Beethoven that we can watch together if you want," I said. This almost made Maxine smile. I had no idea she was such a Beethoven fan.

"Did you know that he was mostly deaf for half of his life?" she said. She clicked a link and Beethoven's "Ode to

Joy" started playing. "He still wrote music, still played and conducted, but could only hear the notes muffled, like they were underwater."

"Sometimes people are really driven to do something, even if they can't fully experience it." I wasn't sure how I came up with this explanation. It was probably one of the most profound things I ever said to her. Most of the time, I felt uncertain talking to her, like someone miscast in a school play. Suddenly, I felt myself getting choked up.

"I think you're starting to understand me," she said.

I wiped the unexpected tears from my eyes and she leaned in to look at me closer. She was smiling widely, open-mouthed, like her mom. I could tell she was going to laugh. "Don't laugh at me," I said.

She laughed and I laughed and we wrestled around, trying to make the other stop laughing. The computer started playing Beethoven's Fifth Symphony. We crouched like fighters, facing each other, our eyes electric, new, and shiny. It was so serious and dramatic.

...

You said your body felt like it had been tapped out and drained—a pipe winding through you, a faucet turned on. "A gushing of blood and fluid like an elephant birth," you actually said.

We had just seen a video of a baby elephant being born. "It's not unusual for the mother to kick the baby around until it breathes," the voiceover said. "The mother trumpets loudly and nudges the newborn until it is able to stand and feed."

You almost started crying as we were watching it. "Sometimes mothers can be monsters," you said.

"They're animals," I said. "They don't know what they're doing."

. . .

Sometimes I wondered if I was teaching Vince enough about life stuff. Like laundry, dishes, cooking eggs, and how much toilet paper to use. My parents were stricter with me, and made me mop and dust and garden and also wash the family car all the time. I learned hospital corners on the bed and how to cook something medium rare. They even made me squeegee the car windows when we stopped for gas. But I failed at grocery shopping for some reason. Always got the wrong cheese or milk. Couldn't make myself buy wheat bread as a child.

Maybe I was too relaxed with Vince, like I wanted to be the cool dad. I would tell him ten more minutes on his video game and let him play for thirty. I would ask him to help with cleaning the bathroom but do most of it myself while he wiped the sink out over and over.

Then I had sudden bouts of guilt about my non-structure, his lack of chores. It became a strange, double-sided guilt. I felt guilty for wanting him to have fun, and I felt guilty for not preparing him for future responsibilities.

One day, I made him iron our nice shirts and pants. I made him spray and wipe off the TV screen. I showed him exactly how long to cook corn on the cob. I even taught him how to log in to the websites for the cable and electric bills and pay them with my bank card.

Before it was time for bed, I remembered one last thing that I'd never shown him: how to change a lightbulb. For some reason, this task made me especially nervous, like he was going to get electrocuted or something. I mean, I don't even know how electricity works.

I pulled the small ladder out and had him climb up and twist the old bulb out. I showed him how to shake it gently and listen for the tiny rattle. I gave him the new one and watched him twist it in. I put my hands on his waist to steady him, though I didn't really need to. I went to bed that night wondering if I had overloaded him with information. If it was too much for his young brain.

I wondered if he'd remember any of these things.

. . .

We were on the bus heading home after a basketball game. It was dark outside and the windows were fogged up. A little girl across from us drew two happy faces on them with her finger. She had on pink fingernail polish and her mom watched her and smiled. They got off at the stop before ours. You scooted over to her happy faces and quickly made bodies for them. One of them was a skinny man with his fist up in the air. A word bubble coming from his mouth said, *Go, Blazers!* You gave the other happy face long hair and the body of a naked woman. Her word bubble said, *Brandon Roy got me pregnant!*

We got off at our stop, making sure to thank the bus driver without looking at him. We ran home like someone was chasing us. Our laughter cut through the fog ahead of us.

...

Maxine wanted a slushie, so she and I got on our bikes and rode down to the mini-mart. When we got there, we found out they didn't have a slushie machine. "I thought all mini-marts were supposed to have slushies," I said.

We rode around some more and found a 7-Eleven, but most of their machines were broken except a flavor we didn't like. "I don't really like Slurpees, anyway," Maxine said. I asked her about the difference between slushies and Slurpees. "One of them is like crushed ice and the other one is like snow," she said. As we were getting back on our bikes, a couple of girls from Maxine's school said hi to her. They were leaning against a VW Bug and one of them tossed a cigarette to the side.

"What's going on?" one of them asked Maxine.

"Just looking for a slushie," Maxine said with a dramatic sigh. I thought the girls might laugh or say something mean, but they stood there, looking around like they were suddenly scared. They were probably a year or two older than Maxine, maybe juniors or seniors. For a moment, it was like I was witnessing the kind of dynamic that happened in the high school hallway. I noticed how the girls' demeanor changed when they saw Maxine, like Maxine was more popular than they were or something. I wondered if Maxine was more revered at school than she let on. Maybe she was a bully.

We rode around the streets some more, looking for a good slushie. I pedaled behind Maxine and watched her with new eyes. She was tough, confident, and decisive. The muscles in her legs were tensed like tight ropes and a couple of lines of sweat moved through the dark hair on her arms like snakes through grass.

The next store didn't have slushies either. Or the next. When we finally found one, at a place called Qwik-Stop, we mixed up the flavors, layering them in our cups and then dipping the scoop-like straw into them.

We leaned against our bikes outside and I asked how her slushie was. "It kind of sucks," she said. I offered a trade, and she took mine. "Yours is a lot better," she said, and I let her keep it. I asked her who the girls at the other store were. "I think one of them is named Daria, but I don't really know," said Maxine.

We got back on our bikes and rode in the direction of home. I was still trailing behind her when she looked back and said, "Hey, thanks."

"What?" I said.

"I'm glad we kept looking," she said. "It was worth it."

...

I had started giving Vince driving lessons when he was fourteen. We'd circle around the huge empty parking lot of a closed-down high school. He was about a year too young to get his permit at that point, but I wanted him to get a head start.

I remember getting my first driving lessons from my grandfather when I was ten. He'd put me in his lap and let me steer as he worked the gas and brake pedals. I wasn't tall enough to drive his car by myself then, but I was allowed to putter around on his riding lawnmower when my parents weren't around. It had a clutch and could go up to twenty miles per hour, though it felt more like fifty. I once rolled it down a hill and broke my arm.

I didn't tell Vince about that though.

We were driving my old Ford Fiesta, which was probably a good size for him, not too big or powerful. We drove in big circles and I'd tell him, "Turn right. Turn left. Try to park between those lines."

By the third or fourth lesson, I felt like he was getting pretty comfortable, and I let him turn the radio on. I tested his multitasking by having him change the station and turn the defroster on while driving in a figure eight. He barely missed one of the lampposts.

"Okay, okay," I said, and pointed to a spot to park in. I got out of the car and told him he could drive by himself around the parking lot for five minutes. "Don't go over thirty-five," I said. It was like a trust exercise.

I watched him cautiously drive around. I saw his face and could tell he was trying to look serious, but there was a smile pushing through. After five minutes, I jumped into his path and made him brake quickly. He was coming right at me, wheels screeching, and my heart sped up. He gripped the steering wheel in a chokehold as the car halted just before my knees.

From the look on Vince's face, I could tell he'd thought he hit me, but I flashed him a quick thumbs-up like I wasn't worried at all. I wanted him to feel like he had control.

. . .

Highway 101 was the slow way, the scenic route. We had three days away from the kids, so we decided to head south and maybe find a way out of the rain. The radio was on and we hadn't spoken since stopping for gas. We were on a mapless, wordless journey.

"You went on a road trip with her, too, didn't you?" you asked, though I didn't really know about whom—maybe Sheryl, maybe one of the girls I'd dated when we were separated.

"I went to dinner with her," I said. "I went to movies, grocery stores, art galleries, car washes, the dentist, and the foot-massaging place with her."

"You went to the dentist with her?" you said back. You turned down the radio.

"I don't know who you're talking about, but yes, I have gone to places with other people."

"Not when you were with me, though," you said. Your seat was pushed all the way back and your feet were braced against the glove box. Your knees were straight and locked hard. I felt the fresh air get sucked out of the car through the whistling crack of the window. We were stuck, even though the car moved forward with us in it. It was a southbound machine, barely slowing for the curves. *What are we doing inside of this thing?* I wondered.

"Bringing it up is not going to help," I answered. "Thinking about it is not going to help. There's no reason to think about that now." I reached over and grabbed your hand, which felt shriveled and reluctant.

"I'm sorry," you said a few minutes later, and your hand opened like a yawn.

"I'm sorry," I said back.

I turned the music back up. We were passing some place called Fort Dick. I was trying to think of something else to talk about. Eventually we'd have to pick a place to turn around. There were trees on each side of us, squeezing our breath out.

...

One of the very first times we were together, it was the day after a snowstorm and there was ten inches of snow on the ground. We took separate buses and met at a café, but it was closed. We decided to walk somewhere else but decided that we should go through a neighborhood where there would be less traffic. We were beginning our affair and didn't want any of our friends to see us. But I couldn't wait to kiss you and hold you, so I turned around and faced you as we walked down a residential street. Somehow we kissed and walked at the same time—me backward, you forward. We opened our coats and looped our arms around each other. I didn't know if people were watching us through their windows, or if anyone would care. We were careless in that moment, something in us releasing forever. We walked like that for three whole blocks, the snow already melting around us.

I don't think we were really concerned about getting caught right then. We knew it wouldn't matter in the end.

...

We went out to a Christmas tree farm. Me, you, and the kids. They gave us all saws and we cut down a medium-size Douglas fir for the front room and two small ones for Vince's and Maxine's bedrooms. The husband and wife who ran the farm gave us all Costco-brand hot chocolate with cheap marshmallows. They were selling decorations too, but they were old and dusty-looking, like they'd belonged to someone's greatgrandmother. The wife talked a lot and said they had run the farm for thirty years now, after taking it over from his father. The husband didn't say much, just smoked his pipe and nodded and smiled at us.

On the drive home, Vince said he had to go to the bathroom. We were about fifteen minutes outside of town, on some old road surrounded by wilderness. It was getting dark and I thought it would be fun to pee in the woods. I didn't think I had ever peed outside with Vince before. It seemed like something he should do with his father.

We pulled over and you gave me a funny look. You turned to Maxine with a grin and said, "You ready for a hillbilly bathroom break?"

I put the parking lights on and we ventured a few yards into the trees. The moon gave us just enough light to see. "Girls over there and boys over here," I said, pointing out some shadowy spots. We each unbuckled and unzipped behind our trees. We relieved ourselves in silence, without making jokes or scary sounds. I wondered if any animals were out there, close to us, watching us. Could they hear our legs snapping through the brush like some kind of unknown creature? Eight legs, eight arms, four hearts.

As we walked back to the car, we started howling at the moon, louder and louder. We gulped the cold fog. We scared the darkness. We laughed.

I hoped that Vince and Maxine would remember this when they were old, and maybe talk about it at some Christmas dinner.

...

We almost didn't get to this point. On one of those first nights, when we were still married to other people, you tried to break it off and I wailed uncontrollably in the front seat of your car. I was surprising even myself by how badly I was taking it. My sobs were almost too loud for the car, but you were trying to calm me down. We were parked three blocks from my apartment.

"Don't cry," you said. "You're going to make me cry, and I don't like to cry over people."

I wasn't sure what you meant by that, and I remember that it almost made me angry. I thought, *What the hell do you cry over then?*

We did end it that night. Only to start it again three days later.

I've seen you cry a lot since then. Over people, animals, TV commercials, sports highlights, food, clothes, car repairs, weather, haircuts, and other things. If I had any doubt about you having a heart or being open with your emotions, those doubts didn't last.

Now it's five years later. I want to pause for a second and think about all we've done. Like a moment of silence before our noise starts up again.

# ACKNOWLEDGMENTS

Writing this book was a great and sometimes strange adventure for me. It seemed to come out of nowhere and take on a life (or lives) of its own. Along the way, I was encouraged, inspired, pushed, influenced, and supported by many friends.

Thank you, Amy Temple Harper. Thank you, Chloe Caldwell. Thank you, Zachary Schomburg. Thank you, Mike Daily. Thank you, Mom. Thank you, Matt Sampsell.

Gratitude and love: Jamie Iredell, Andrew Monko, Elizabeth Ellen, Stephen Kurowski, Reuben Nisenfeld, Michael Heald, Susie Bright, Gregory Sherl, Dena Rash Guzman, Magdalen Powers, and the Taxidermy gang: especially Matt Brown, Pauls Toutonghi, Emily Kendal Frey, and Arthur Bradford.

Thanks to Bryan Coffelt and the rest of my Future Tense Books family.

Eternal thanks to my Powell's Books family.

For Davy, Amelia, Jillian, Jess, Patrick, and Lidia. I admire you all.

For B. Frayn Masters, the love that never stops. You have always been there and have always believed in me—and in this book—even when I wasn't sure what the heck I was doing.

For Zacharath, my heart.

Thank you to my dream editor, Masie Cochran. My Tin House posse: Nanci, Tony, Meg, Jakob, Diane, Desiree, and everyone else (Cindy Heidemann! XO!).

And thank *you*, especially, reader. Thank you so much.